MASTER ENTRICK

OTHER YEARLING BOOKS YOU WILL ENJOY:

MASTER ENTRICK

AN ADVENTURE
1754~1756

BY
MICHAEL MOTT

A YEARLING BOOK

Published by
Dell Publishing Co., Inc.
1 Dag Hammarskjold Plaza
New York, New York 10017

This work was first published in Great Britain by Andre Deutsch
Limited, London.

Yearling ® TM 913705, Dell Publishing Co., Inc.

ISBN: 0-440-45818-8

Reprinted by arrangement with Delacorte Press

Printed in the United States of America

One Previous Yearling Edition

October 1986

10 9 8 7 6 5 4 3 2 1

CW

Contents

CHARACTERS

ROBERT ENTRICK	*A boy*
THOMAS ENTRICK	*His uncle*
THE BIRDTAKER	*Criminal and, later, soldier*
BEN	*Criminal*
CAPTAIN MASK	*Captain of* The Charming Betty
THE NEWT	*An indentured servant of twelve*
HANNAH	*An Irish indentured servant*
MASSEY	*An impressed seaman, former silversmith, later a publican*
CALVIN MOORE	*A Colonial farmer*
AGATHA	*Calvin's second wife*
THE BUTTERFIELDS	*A Colonial family*
HENRY BENTALL	*Colonist, former schoolmaster*
JACOB	*Colonist*
HE-WHO-HAS-KILLED-A-BEAR	*An Indian boy*
I-SMILE-THOUGH-I-AM-IN-MOURNING	*His mother*
BLACK SWAN	*His grandmother*
BEAK-OF-THE-EAGLE	*His father, chief of the tribe*
BRIGHT DAWN	*His uncle*
JOHN LAWRENCE	*Lieutenant in the British Army*
MATHEW LAWRENCE	*His father, an attorney*
MRS. JARROW	*Housekeeper of Thomas Entrick at Tice Hall*

❧ 1 ❧

"The World Turned Upside Down"

ON THURSDAY, NOVEMBER 14, 1754, Thomas Entrick rode over to Bower in Lancashire to post in the taproom of The Loyalist and in the church porch the following notice:

> REWARD!!!—To any who have heard of or seen Master Robert Entrick, the nephew of Thomas Entrick Esq., of Tice Hall in the Parish of Holywell, after last Friday, the eighth day of November; or who can give evidence, advice or information as to his present whereabouts, whether he be ALIVE or DEAD, A REWARD OF TWENTY GUINEAS will be paid at the hand of the said Thomas Entrick Esq., or of his Attorney-at-Law, Walter Breame, at 14, The High Street, Bower.

At dusk on the Friday before the posting of this notice Robert was on his way home from school. Each morning and evening, summer and winter when it was term-time, he rode this same rough track for three miles over the moorland between the Hall and his school in the village of Holywell.

For part of the way (the stretch he was now riding) the path ran along the spine of a long ridge of almost bare rock. When he had the time on a clear day he would stop the pony here and look far to the north and west over the Yorkshire dales.

But on that cold, blustering evening the twilight had fallen early. It was almost dark by now and even the landscape near him was blurred. The wind had grown stronger while he rode and it gave the countryside a strange life of its own. Robert knew every clump of bushes on the way. It did not startle him, as it might have done a stranger, to see a dark shape, still until then, rise up in the half-light like a rearing horse, then fall away just as suddenly and disappear altogether.

There was nothing to be afraid of, he knew that. He had been out on worse nights than this. Even so, as he rode he thought of the old stories of the Scots, of Black Douglas raiding and the Moss Troopers who had ridden as quiet as ghosts over the Border. It was easy on such a night to hear things behind the wind.

He tried to fix his thoughts on the Hall. In another half hour he would be there, sitting by the warm fire waiting for his supper; the high wind and the darkness of the night would be shut outside the thick walls of the house.

At that moment he heard a sharp, shrill whistle. It was quite close and it sounded like a man calling his dog to heel.

He had come to the part of the track that ran down steeply between the walls of granite from the high ridge to the dale. The last of the daylight was blotted out by the cliffs and the sound of the wind dropped away abruptly to a low moan, like a draft behind a closed door.

Here the whistle came again, louder this time and closer still—it seemed to start from somewhere in the darkness at the other end of the gorge. It sounded insistent now, almost mocking.

Robert's heart was hammering. He wondered whether to turn and ride back. But something in the whistling itself appeared to draw him on. He wondered, too, if it could be one of the stable boys coming to meet him and trying to frighten him. If he ran they would laugh at him for weeks.

There was a third whistle; now it seemed almost chiding

him for holding back. He was halfway along the scar of rock.

Not one but two figures on horseback came up out of the darkness toward him. The pony and the horses were almost touching heads when again Robert heard the whistling. This time it was very low, as though the whistler were whistling to himself. "Easy, laddie, go easy," a voice said, a voice Robert had never heard before.

At the last moment he tried to turn the pony. As he did so someone made a grab at his reins, missed and cursed. The narrow gorge was full of turning and plunging horses. For a second Robert thought he had broken free. Then he saw something raised above his head. Before he had time to duck the blow struck him, jarring his teeth together and knocking him sideways. Someone caught him and held him up for a moment. At his ear, softly, almost playfully spoken, he heard the words "Aye then, the bird taken and never a wing broken."

The voice was gentle, persuasive, but for the first time a wave of terror passed over Robert. He carried his fear with him as he slipped sideways into the darkness, groping for the ground but finding nothing. The whole familiar world seemed to topple with him.

2

The Birdtaker

THERE WAS NOTHING to tell Robert how long he had been unconscious or asleep—it might have been for a day or more. He had been dreaming that he was back at the Hall; that Mrs. Jarrow, the housekeeper, had been arguing with his uncle over letting him ride home from school on his own on such an evening. He dreamed she had taken his coat from him, sat him down among cushions in the big chimney corner by the fire and brought him his food where he sat in the warmth with the two dogs lying at his feet.

Now that he was wide awake for the first time he glanced around to see where he was. It was still fairly dark, but the light came through holes in the covering overhead—enough to show it was daytime outside and that he was lying in what looked like the back of a large covered farm wagon among crates and boxes.

His head ached with a continuous throbbing pain from the sore spot where he had been struck. His arms were tied awkwardly behind his back and he was doubled up, his knees brought close to his chest, squeezed into a narrow space between two crates.

A few minutes after he woke up, the flaps at the rear of the wagon were pulled open and the daylight flooded in. Robert heard someone climb in and move behind his back. He felt a tugging at the ropes that bound his arms; something cut through them and his arms were free.

When Robert turned over, a short, ugly man of fifty or more was kneeling beside him. The man's neck and chin were covered with white stubble. His mouth, full of crooked black teeth, was set at an angle. His eyes were bright and the deep wrinkles around them made him look as though he were laughing, if only at some cruel joke of his own.

As soon as he spoke Robert recognized the voice of the whistler in the gorge. There was the same softness in his voice—it was almost a whisper—and there was the same tone of pretended friendliness.

"Come out and stretch your limbs, Johnnie-boy," the man said cheerfully. At the same time he wiped a long, curved knife with which he had cut the ropes carefully across the upper of one of his boots, then put it away in a sheath that hung at his side. After this he climbed back over the tailboard of the wagon and disappeared. Robert first hesitated, then followed him.

The wagon was standing in a wood by a lake. Snow lay several inches deep on the ground and it covered the branches of the trees. Two horses were drinking at the edge of the water, one dun-colored, the other black. Some way off a small fire was burning, looking like a black smudge on the almost perfect surface of the snow, a smudge with a small yellow center. On a fallen tree beside the fire sat a second man wrapped in a gray blanket. There was a pot on a spit over the fire, and steam came out of the top. The air was cold and clear. The sun was up and it shone brightly on the white snow and the white water.

As Robert walked awkwardly with stiff, aching limbs across the snow to the fire he heard something which made him stop and look around in all directions. It had been very still until that moment, then, all of a sudden, a birdcall had started up, shrill and clear in the cold air. Robert searched the snow and the nearest branches. The bird could not be far—and yet there was no sign of it!

"Oh, give it a rest, why don't you!" the man in the gray

blanket said, showing a heavy-featured, morose face when he looked up to speak.

The smaller man, who stood close to Robert, gave a laugh. "Blackbird," he announced. The minute he caught Robert's eye he winked broadly, then pursed his lips. From his mouth trill upon trill of bird notes fountained forth in a thin, clear, bubbling stream. Something bubbled too in the old man's throat and in his cheeks, but in spite of this what came from his mouth seemed quite divorced from him. The birdcall soared up and up, higher and higher, until it broke away abruptly, ending in a grotesque, very human chuckle. "Skylark," the old man said triumphantly. He glanced at Robert again and was rewarded by a look of astonishment.

"Ben here's no love for warblers, have you, Ben? No delicate ear. But if I catch a rabbit while he sits ruminating there, then he'll oblige me by eating it. Come and see, boy."

Robert followed the strange man as he walked a hundred or so yards from the fire. Here, quite plain in the snow, the tracks of a rabbit first meandered about, then set off in a straight line. The tracks of a man came out from behind a row of trees to meet them. Where they met, the rabbit's tracks stopped; the man's returned the way they had come.

At the meeting place the old man squatted down low in the snow. He began to make soft, slight sounds in his throat, sounds that seemed to be imploring something to come to him. With one hand he acted out the rabbit's cautious approach; then, with the other, the quick, timed lunge at the animal's neck. When the mime was over he broke the spell with another chuckle and looked up at Robert for approval.

Robert said nothing, but again his expression was enough to please the man. As they walked back he said, "There's many fowlers and such that laugh at them that say there's no need to know the language and put their trust in traps and lures, mirrors and lime and all manner of things to take game. But where's the sense in piking all this about when you have what my father taught me? Thirty years now I've been a birdtaker, thirty years or more, boy, and that rabbit came to me like his own true love."

His boasting, his almost childish display of his skill, all his pretended friendliness only made Robert dislike him more. He might have asked the bigger man called Ben outright what they were doing with him, why they had taken him from his home, where they were going; but something cautioned Robert to wait, to study the Birdtaker closely for some time before he trusted himself even to speak to him. The moment when this man had cut through his bonds with a knife only an inch or so from his back returned to Robert and he shuddered.

The Birdtaker was slipping the same long, curved knife into the pot on the fire. He brought out a square of brown meat dripping with rich stock, cooled it and then slipped it into his mouth. "It's rum prog," he pronounced. "Let's eat."

They ate with their fingers and with lumps of a coarse brown bread, which the Birdtaker divided up among them. The rabbit meat came easily away from the bones, and the rich, sweet juice mixed with stock stuck to their fingers and had to be licked free.

"It's cold enough," Ben said when they were finished, pulling the blanket up. "Cold, perishing cold! Can't you do nothing with that fire!"

The Birdtaker chuckled maliciously. Instead of stirring the fire, he got up quickly to his feet. "Time to be off!" he said; and he kicked the snow over the embers, which sizzled, steamed, spluttered and died. Although he cursed him, Ben got up, picked up the spit and the iron pot and shambled off back to the wagon.

When Robert returned to the wagon, Ben was trying to hitch the two horses to the traces and the dun was giving trouble. He called on Robert to help him. Working together, they succeeded in backing the big horse into place, but Robert fumbled with the harness, having no idea what to do with it. "Proper little lord, aren't you?" Ben said. "Proper little Marmaduke. Oh, they'll change the style of your rig for you—you wait!" He gave Robert a buffet with his arm that sent him crashing hard against the side of the wagon.

"Leave the boy be, Ben!" the Birdtaker said in his quiet, cold voice. Neither of them had seen him come up while they had been working. "Take yourself off if it's too much for you outside. There's a fine warm sty in the back there for a pig to wallow in."

He slurred over the last words in a way that brought Ben up as though he had been slapped with a glove. The bigger man strode over and stood menacing the Birdtaker, a head and shoulders taller than he was. Robert waited for a blow that never came. A moment later Ben shambled off to the back as he had been ordered. They heard him pitch himself clumsily into the inside of the wagon.

"Come up then, boy, look sharp!" the Birdtaker said. He gave Robert a push onto the high driving board of the wagon, then went around to the far side and hoisted himself up. Once in his seat, he cracked the whip and started up the horses. They left the lakeside and soon joined what appeared to be an important road from the milestones under white nightcaps of snow which they passed. All traces of the road itself had been erased, and Robert looked at the landscape with despair. Even if he had an opportunity of breaking away from these two, how would he ever find his way back?

For a while the Birdtaker continued to abuse Ben. At any minute Robert expected the bigger man to tear open the cover at their back and pitch them both from the driving board. Nothing happened, however. Finally, getting no response from either of his companions, the old man started to sing to himself.

"I am a gay young spark . . ." he began in a somewhat reedy voice, and as he continued Robert recognized the words of a song that had recently become popular and that some called "The World Turned Upside Down" and others "Money Grown Troublesome" but that everyone—his father,

Robert remembered, like the Birdtaker at that moment—sang to an old air the country fiddlers had played since time immemorial, "Packington's Pound."

A mile or so farther on they came to a river running black and full through the white landscape. The wagon pitched and heaved going over the humpback bridge. On the other side there was a signpost pointing to Liverpool.

❧ 3 ❧

Sold

EARLY ON THE SAME EVENING they came into a large town. There was hardly a light to be seen, but an almost full moon shone on the black fronts of the buildings and on the white street, the white rooftops, chimneys, gables and ledges. This was the first time Robert had been in anything larger than a small market town. Sitting on the driving seat of the wagon beside the Birdtaker and looking about, he felt a great wave of depression, as though the dark, unbroken silhouettes of the houses on either side were high walls blocking out his last hope of escape.

At a crossroads where bright panels of light shone out over the trampled snow a crowd of people had gathered, shouting, singing in maudlin voices, holding one another up. Robert could see the upturned faces, close to him, lit by the lamplight. He was on the point of calling out for help, but something told him he would get no help here. When the Birdtaker stood up and brandished the whip, the crowd fell back against the wall, shouting up, not angrily, for them to stop and "drink a health to the white bantam." But as the wagon drew away the crowd followed it with cries of derision.

The Birdtaker had been silent for hours. Twice during the day Robert had made an attempt to draw out of him why they had taken him from his home and what they were going to do with him. Each time the Birdtaker had chuckled and clucked his tongue. "We're taking you from your school, boy, to show you the wide world," he said the second time Robert asked. But he let it be known that was all he would say on the subject. For much of the day he had sung or whistled "The World Turned Upside Down" over and over to himself. At other times he had talked of his skill, as though he were teaching Robert his trade. Now the man might have been asleep, except that his eyes were open and his small hands were firm on the reins.

Of Ben nothing had been seen all day except when they had stopped near noon at an inn. Then Ben had shambled out, more animal-like than ever, disappeared for a moment inside and come out with a bottle in each hand. With these he had climbed into the back once more without so much as a glance at the others.

Now, in the town, the road began to go downhill. In the gap ahead between the houses Robert saw something that caught his attention. Tall spars and crisscross patterns stood out against the moonlit sky, and with a shock Robert realized that he was looking at the ships he had seen before only in pictures.

The sight appeared to waken the Birdtaker beside him. He began to look about, and then turned the horses into a side alley that would only just take the width of the wagon. Halfway along this alley a faint light glowed green through four panes of a mullioned window. Close to this light the Birdtaker drew up the horses and got down.

When the Birdtaker had squeezed his way around the side of the wagon to wake Ben, Robert found himself on his own. The alleyway ahead seemed to be free and it appeared to lead to another road. Here was his chance!

His heart pounding, Robert tied the reins to a clamp and slid off the wagon. Once on the ground, he stood and listened. He hesitated for a minute longer, uncertain where to go. He decided, just on a slight chance of finding help to run to the inn where the crowd had called out to them.

But he had been too slow and it was too late. A hand closed on his shoulder. "Why'd you get down—eh?" the Birdtaker asked in a whisper.

"My feet were cold," Robert said quickly, expecting a cuff or worse. Instead the Birdtaker turned and led the way into the inn; the others followed.

From the doorway a low passage just wide enough to take a man's shoulders led past three paneled booths which were crowded to bursting point. The men who stood packed together in the booths drinking from black leather cans were dressed in the roughest of clothes, some in layer upon layer of crudely stitched canvas, others in darned and patched jackets of blue, or red and white stripes. Many of the last had pigtails that stuck out straight from the backs of their heads and gold earrings in their ears.

But Robert hardly had time to look about before Ben pushed him on down the passage until it broadened out into a larger room that seemed empty except for great piles of furniture. At the far end of this room a man stood holding a lantern above an open trap door in the floor. He beckoned them on. The Birdtaker went down the ladder first through the trap. Ben pushed Robert after him, but remained upstairs himself.

By the light of the lantern Robert could see the cellar below as he climbed down into it. A great heap of straw lay in the middle of the floor, and scattered over this, looking like tramps in a hayrick, were four, five, six people, asleep, or pretending to be.

When he reached the bottom, Robert noticed that one of the figures in the straw, a boy of about his own age, had opened his eyes. He blinked at the lantern, looked curiously at Robert for a full minute, then closed his eyes again.

The Birdtaker returned to the ladder and climbed up again, closing the trap door behind him at the top.

After standing for a moment anxious and uncertain what

to do, Robert felt his way back, in the darkness, to the pile of straw, careful not to step on anyone lying there. He sat down and waited. The straw felt damp and smelled musty; but it was the sense of dread inside Robert that now made him feel almost sick.

A few minutes later the trap door was opened and three people came down the ladder into the cellar—first the Bird-taker with the lantern, then a stranger in a blue uniform, and finally Ben. Ben waved about violently, almost missing his footing. At the bottom he sat down on a low rung and gazed hard at the light and at the people in the straw.

The man dressed in blue came over at once to Robert. Robert got to his feet, but the man stood in front of him and stared at him without saying a word.

The first thing Robert noticed about the stranger was that there was something unnatural about his face. The skin was taut, as yellow as cheap tallow, and it seemed to shine strangely in the light. A black mat of hair fitted his head too neatly, with a hard line, so that it looked as though he had on a black wool cap. In the artificial-looking face the eyes were sunk in deep sockets, but they were bright and there was no escape from their fixed gaze.

"He's a mere boy," the man in blue said, speaking not to Robert, at whom he continued to stare, but to the Birdtaker, standing behind him.

"But I said he was, sir," the Birdtaker replied.

"You said nothing of the kind," the stranger said crisply.

There was a pause, but all the time the man kept Robert under his cold, steady gaze. "Thirty guineas!" he rapped out after minutes of silence.

"Be blowed!" Ben cried out. "Thirty guineas be blowed!" He came suddenly to life, stumbled up from the seat in a gathering rage and closed on the stranger. "Thirty!" he bellowed in the man's ear. He raised his clenched fists above the stranger's head.

"Get this thing away from me!" the man in the blue coat said, not bothering to turn to face his assailant and speaking all the time to the Birdtaker.

"Pike to the dancers, Ben buff!" the Birdtaker ordered quietly. He plucked Ben's coat by the sleeve and half dragged him away to the foot of the ladder.

"Thirty, thirty. Risk getting turned off at some highwayman's gallows . . ." Ben shouted; but there was more whine than bellow now in his slurred voice. "Risk all that for thirty guineas! Two days waiting and that old idiot who couldn't make up his mind how he wanted things . . ."

"Give your tongue a rest, you fool!" the Birdtaker said, his voice no more than actor's aside this time, his words for Ben's ears alone. At the sound of them, however, the last of Ben's bluster disappeared, leaving no trace. He crumpled up, took his seat once more on the ladder, buried his big, shaggy head in his hands and scrubbed his scalp with his fingers. "*You* do it then," he said.

"Thirty's very little sir," the Birdtaker began again gently, as though Ben's fury had made no interruption in their conversation.

"You'll take it if you've any sense," the stranger said. "This is no mudlark you've brought me. No plowboy either. He may not last the passage. What sort of bargain have I then?" The man looked into Robert's face again as if to reassure himself. "He's gentry, isn't he? You'll have been paid once already, like as not, unless you're a pair of real fools. Thirty, I say. No more."

"Fifty . . ." the Birdtaker tried.

"Thirty!" The man dressed in blue turned on his heel quickly, as though to be off; but at that moment the Birdtaker nodded agreement and he turned back to face Robert. He drew out a small notebook and pencil from one of his pockets and flicked the book open.

"What's your name, lad?" he asked, addressing Robert for the first time.

"Robert Entrick, sir, of Tice Hall, near Bower . . ." Robert started, but he had no time to finish. The man reached out and tapped him on the head. There was a ring on the finger that struck Robert's scalp, and the blow was hard enough to bring tears of pain shooting up into his eyes. He had to fight with himself to keep his bearing.

"Your name," the stranger said without lifting his voice, "is Jack Allen and where you came from nobody cares. Look here . . ." He thrust the notebook into Robert's face. "I'm writing it down in my book—Jack Allen. If you forget that name, then I'll teach you to remember no other."

With a quick, precise movement he flicked the notebook shut and out of sight again. Then he turned smartly and walked off. On his way out he pushed Ben off the ladder and out of his way with a rough jab of his hand. Ben picked himself up from the floor and followed without even a curse. Only the Birdtaker turned back before leaving for a moment. He stood holding the light at the foot of the ladder, the same fixed grin set on his twisted face that he had worn on that morning when Robert saw him for the first time. "Well, Jack boy," he said by way of parting, "good luck and no hard thoughts—eh?" With this he climbed and disappeared. The ladder was dragged up after him; the trap door was slammed down and bolted with a noise that vibrated through the black cellar.

4

The Newt

STANDING THERE in complete darkness, rubbing his head to take away the stinging pain from the blow the stranger had given him, Robert felt a sudden wave of anger. Since that moment when he had been ambushed in the gorge everyone had treated him like a lunatic or a wild animal. Was everyone going to treat him like this from now on? And why? As far as he knew he hadn't changed. He was exactly the same person. Why did everyone think they could abuse him?

And why had he come so tamely into a place like this? Why had he been so slow when at least there had been a chance to escape? There was no chance here; he was trapped in this damp black hole for as long as they wanted to keep him.

"Are you there, sir?" came a whisper behind him. "The Captain himself came down for you, sir—the Captain himself!"

Robert turned around, but there was nothing to be seen in the darkness, not even an outline. He remembered the boy who had stared at him when he first came down into the cellar. He knew nothing about him—he could hardly remember what he looked like—but at least the voice was friendly.

"What Captain?" Robert whispered back.

"Why, Captain Mask, sir," the other voice answered from the darkness. "I know him. He was pointed out to me on the dock," the voice said, sounding very full of pride and awe. "I know Captain Mask all right, the gentleman in the blue coat who spoke to you, sir." Then after a pause, he asked "Are you for America, then, begging your pardon, sir?"

"Am I what?" Robert said.

"Going to the Colonies with Captain Mask. To New York."

A chill feeling had come over Robert. There was no answer he could make, but the other boy spoke again almost immediately in the same urgent breathless whisper: "Your friends arranged the passage for you with the Captain."

"My friends?" Robert said, even more startled.

"The two gentlemen with you . . ."

Did he mean the Birdtaker and Ben? His friends! If the other boy was so wrong about this, he could be wrong about everything.

"Where are *you* going?" Robert asked him.

There was a pause—such a long pause that Robert thought he was not going to answer; then came a whispered rush of chatter spoken so fast the boy had to catch his breath at a gulp as he went in order to get out all he wanted to say in the single outburst: "Me, sir? To the American colonies. I've my passage agreed between the Alderman and Captain Mask to go on his ship, sir, *The Charming Betty,* sir, tomorrow on the tide, they say. We're to go overseas and we're to have masters for seven years like apprentices, sir, to pay for the passage. But they are all very rich in America—all lords our masters are to be, sir. And we are to live in houses, very big. And there is no winter there to speak of. Quite warm it will be by report. And no prisons. And if we work our hardest we shall do what we like and go into parks and the houses of the very richest. At the end of seven years, they say, if we are good and have worked with a will, we shall be given a golden guinea and may be masters ourselves if we choose to be."

All this came out in such a tumble Robert got no sense from any of it, but the other boy's excitement made Robert so merry he laughed outright.

There was a groan from nearby. "Hush your blasted prattle, you gallow's brats, or I'll break your bones!" a man's voice said.

"Who's that?" Robert whispered.

"We'd best be quiet," his companion whispered back, so softly Robert could hardly catch his words. "He nearly crippled me once for talking up on the way here and would do it again, your worship. We'd best wait till morning if you please."

Robert heard him drawing himself quietly away through the straw. He felt alone again when the other boy had gone, but their conversation had made him gay and lighthearted. Robert had decided nothing the boy said made any sense, but he was looking forward to seeing him again in the morning.

It was not for a few hours of darkness, however, but for a night and most of the following day that Robert and his companions were kept in the cellar. During this time nobody visited them.

To pass the time Robert tried to sleep. But he had slept for too much of the period since his capture, and now he lay awake with no way of counting the hours except for a growing hunger. In this long ordeal of darkness and silence it helped him to know that someone he knew and had spoken to lay not far away from him in the same darkness.

When he was not thinking of their talk Robert tried to imagine what they would be saying about his mysterious disappearance back at his school and at the Hall. He wondered how many of his school friends would miss him. For a moment he shut his eyes and remembered every detail of the classroom; then he imagined the headmaster making the announcement that Master Entrick could not be found. Would they think he had been killed? Or that he had run away?

Who would miss him at home?

His mother had died so early in his life that he had no

memory of her. When his father had been in the house the
Hall had resounded with his loud voice, his laughter, his
footsteps, which had seemed twice as heavy as those of anyone
else. But these visits were rare and had lasted for only a few
weeks on each occasion, before his father rode off again to the
wars in the Low Countries. Then the day had come when a
stranger rode in bearing on his horse a bundle of clothes from
which the hilts of two swords stuck out and a small chest
bound in iron with his father's initials set in nails. Robert
knew, long before his Uncle Thomas had told him, that his
father was dead. His uncle had taken his father's things to
keep for him until he was old enough to have them.

His uncle might miss him. Thomas Entrick was a stern
man, usually silent, who kept to himself in his own rooms at
the Hall, as different from his older brother, Robert's father,
as it was possible for brothers to be. But he had never spoken
unkindly to Robert, except once when Robert had gone to
his room unasked and he had flown into an odd rage. Otherwise he had given Robert ponies to ride, hawks and dogs to
hunt with; and he had always allowed him to do much as he
wanted.

Mrs. Jarrow, the housekeeper, would miss him, he was sure
of that. For the last four years she had looked after him when
he needed help, taught him his manners, kept his clothes in
order, nursed him when he had been ill after falling out of a
tree trying to recapture a favorite hawk. But he remembered
that she seldom spoke to him for long and always appeared to
be preoccupied with other things when he most needed her.

If he could have gone back at that moment disguised or
invisible, he would have walked through the great hall where
Jupiter and Juno, the staghounds, lay for most of the day,
stretched out, enormous by the fireplace; gone into the
kitchen where huge hams and bunches of brown herbs hung
from the beams; climbed the broad staircase to the long
passage upstairs that smelled of wax and lavender; gone on
into his own room and lain down there on his own familiar

bed, listening perhaps for a long time to the noises from the stables and the park . . .

His thoughts were interrupted abruptly by the sound of heavy footsteps overhead. He came back reluctantly from the warm thoughts of the past into the cold present. At that moment the trap door was pulled back, a gray light flooded the cellar, the ladder came down.

A man appeared carrying a bucket in one hand, a large stick thrust under his arm. At the first sight of him the other people in the cellar sprang to life. Hardly had the man reached the floor before they were around him in a crowd. The man with the bucket used his stick freely and shouted to them to get back, but this had very little effect. One bondsman cringed back from the blows, but the others made a still stronger attack. In the end the intruder put down the pail and fled up the ladder.

Robert watched the fight from a distance. He saw several of the men reach their arms into the bucket, draw out chunks of what might have been clay from its color, and thrust whatever they could get into their mouths, not stopping to eat before they were back again fighting for more.

After a while he saw someone push his way out between the legs of two of those in the struggle and make away quickly, his hands full, his head down. He came straight to Robert.

Robert found that his friend was short and thin, a tiny fellow in fact, with an overlarge head, a pointed, hungry face in which two big eyes shone brightly, looking even larger and brighter for the dark circles around them. The boy's face was smeared all over with the same claylike paste that dripped from his fingers.

"Have you a 'kerchief, sir?" he asked Robert.

Searching his pockets, Robert found a big linen handkerchief still folded and clean from the linen cupboard at the Hall. He spread this out on the straw and the other boy emptied his takings into it. As soon as this was done he was off again, wriggling expertly back into the melee around the bucket. Robert watched him, fascinated, but a little disgusted too. He could think of nothing so much as of a mouse or a rat, half expecting to see a tail on the end of his friend. But the boy was back again in a moment with a full load.

"We'd best go around to the other side of the straw, your honor," he said. "The bucket's near enough empty now and I warrant they'll be after us if they see us eating."

They carried the full handkerchief around to the far side of the mound of straw and sat down.

"There's leeks in it and meat," the boy said. "Search about!"

Poor Robert! If it had not been for the fact that he was so hungry and that he was afraid of offending his friend, he would never have touched what he brought. A reek of stale vegetables was coming up from what was disguised with a covering of cold flour paste. However, he picked up one largish gray lump and put this into his mouth without thinking any more about it. It was meat of some sort and still warm. After that he ate his share of what little they had without much difficulty.

The strange little fellow beside him lay back on the straw as though he for one had been quite satisfied by the meal. "They'll bring jars and water soon," he said. "They did yesterday. Then you'd best look sharp yourself, if you'll excuse me saying so, sir, or they'll splash you all over before you've had a drop to swallow. What a rough lot they are here!"

Robert said he would try.

"I knew you'd be at a loss, your honor, the first time, not knowing rightly what to expect. They'll batter you and knock you about if you try to eat properly. You'd best do what I do, sir, go low and trust to luck they don't kick you. That's the way to get your sops and victuals."

"What's your name?" Robert asked.

"They call me the Newt, sir," the boy said. "It's a no-

meaning name, but Newt, or the Newt it is, even in Captain
Mask's book. Once they called me Jeremy Teal," he added
shyly. "What's your name?"

"Robert Entrick," Robert replied, "or Jack . . . or the
Kestrel—you could call me the Kestrel if you wanted to."

"It's best," the other boy said solemnly, accepting this. "It's
best to have a no-meaning name here. What's a kestrel?"

Robert did his best to explain that it was a bird you
trained to hunt other birds, but the Newt seemed to understand very little of what he was saying. He was satisfied,
however, that it was a good enough name to be called by.
"It's best, a no-meaning name," he repeated and again there
was the same note of pride in his voice as though he were
pleased to be showing Robert some secret place in which he
alone was master.

Their conversation was broken off now by a harsh command shouted down from above: "Come out one by one,
below there, and look sharp!"

"We're going!" the Newt said, shivering all over with
excitement. He caught Robert's sleeve and tugged at it.
"Come on!"

"Going where?" Robert said, faltering a little.

"To America! America! America!" the Newt chanted. He
left Robert and almost danced ahead, hurrying to get to the
ladder.

Robert was the last up. He climbed slowly rung by rung,
his head feeling numb with the thoughts the Newt had put
into it. A sailor put his arm around Robert's shoulders near
the top and hoisted him, not unkindly, to the floor.

There were four sailors waiting and a bosun giving orders.
The small party of seven, wretched in their rags, were
marched off single file under the guard, along the passage and
out into the street. Robert saw that it was late in the afternoon on a dull winter day, the sky gray, a large red sun about
to go down behind the houses. Even this much light made

the party from the cellar blink and stumble. The air was
warmer; snow was beginning to thaw from the walls and the
gutters. Several of the party scooped up handfuls of yellow
trodden snow and sucked it.

The strange procession passed along a road, passers-by
paying it little attention. Farther on, the road opened into
what looked like a broad square. Here Robert saw three
ships drawn up on the far side, their masts and rigging rising
high up into the air. The wharf was crowded with people and
cluttered with great piles of stores, timber, and baggage,
looking like the main street of Bower on a market day. The
procession wound its way between walls of barrels, crossed a
plank over water, and found itself on the deck of one of the
ships.

If anything, the deck of the ship was more crowded, busier,
more cluttered than the dock.

"What's this supposed to be?" someone asked at the gangplank.

"The bondsmen. Where are they to go, sir?" the bosun
asked.

"Go? There's no place for them to go till the hold's packed.
Put them fo'r'd of the main hatch and rope them," the officer
said.

Forward they went, picking their way among cases, casks,
hen coops, even two small trees in pots. Ropes were found
and the bondsmen were tied fast to one hawser. They sat
down where they could and waited in the cold damp evening.

For all the discomfort, it was a hundred times better
outside on the deck of the ship than in the cellar. Robert
found so much to watch that a good deal of his anxiety and
hunger seemed to disappear. When he looked at the Newt he
saw him straining forward, his eyes even brighter than usual,
following each coming or going between the ship and the
dock.

A few hours after nightfall there was a swift increase in the

tempo of the loading, and parties of men ran here and there
clearing the deck. Orders and counter-orders were shouted
back and forth. Minutes later, a lull seemed to move back
through the ship. Sailors walked slowly to take up positions
by the side in groups of three or four. Two men walked
aboard and the gangplank was brought in. An order started
at the bow was repeated back. Men shinned swiftly up the
ropes and disappeared into the rigging overhead. Now the air
was filled with orders, cries and curses. Great sheets of canvas
billowed heavily out and seemed to take up the whole sky
over the ship. Ropes screamed through pulleys and blocks,
and the ship itself appeared to come alive underfoot.

Robert was looking up, his attention taken by watching a
sail unfurl, when he was struck violently from behind. He
picked himself up as someone ran past him. He was in time
to see the man strike out at two of the sailors, scramble up
onto the side of the ship, stand for a second tottering and
then disappear overboard. There was a loud splash below.

The group of sailors rushed to the side and peered over.
More sailors came running up and then the bosun.

"Get to the dock and take him!" a voice said quietly but
distinctly. The man speaking walked up and stood a few feet
away from Robert. His features were in the shadow but
Robert had no difficulty in recognizing Captain Mask. "Kill
the idiot if you have to, but get him back aboard, do you hear
me? I want that man. Mr. Mate," he said to the officer standing on the other side of him. "No man jumps my ship. Who
is he?"

"One of the pressed men; no seaman of mine, sir," came the
answer. Orders were given out by the second officer. There
was a sound of footsteps going away down the deck at a run.
"We'll get him for you, sir," the Mate said quietly.

The deck appeared empty now except for the bondsmen
roped together and the two officers standing close to them. It
was strangely quiet apart from the luffing of the sails and a
creaking of ropes. Some time passed, then a shout went up.

"What's that noise down there?" Captain Mask demanded.

The other officer walked to the side. "They've hooked him up for you, sir," the Mate said. The word "hooked," as the Mate said it, made Robert feel cold.

Again there was quiet for a few minutes. Then Robert heard a party coming back along the deck talking noisily among themselves. One of the seamen in the front of the crowd held a lantern. By its light Robert could see they were carrying someone along with them, his feet dragging behind him on the deck and his body dripping a trail of water. His head was down. The party fell silent as they came up to the Captain. One of them lifted the man's head by the hair and another set the lantern close against it so the Captain could see. In the lantern light the face was livid, almost blue, but down one side ran a darker stain. The man's eyes were closed and his mouth hung open.

"Dead?" Captain Mask demanded.

"No, sir," the bosun said. "We caught him a clip with the hook getting him out. He's out cold."

"Take a look at him, Mr. Mate. Is he worth keeping?" Captain Mask said.

The officer stepped forward and looked. "It's a flesh wound, sir."

"Very good," came the Captain's voice again. "Let it mend tonight, but if he wakes this side of Hell tomorrow, work him, Bosun, work him. He owes me an hour of time and tide. Cast off!"

~ 5 ~

The Long Crossing

FROM WHERE HE LAY Robert could imagine that he was back in the hayloft of the great barn at the Hall. He had room to stretch out, and beneath him there was a comfortable layer of fresh straw. His bunk was the second from the top in a set of four, built like wooden shelves against the side of the ship. A large lantern hung above from a hook. This shone night and day, giving a warm light to everything in the hold and constantly changing the pattern of shadows cast by ropes and pieces of rag as it tilted and righted itself with the motion of the ship.

At that moment the lantern was hardly moving. The ship seemed strangely still, as though it had come to anchor in a calm sea. There was no sound except for a subdued noise of water and the steady breathing of the bondsmen in the other bunks. In the bunk above Robert the Newt gave a groan in his sleep and turned over.

Perhaps it was the hour on deck that morning that kept Robert awake, his thoughts moving restlessly back and forth. One minute it depressed him to think that with every mile they traveled he was being drawn further and further from his own life and the chance of returning to it. But the next minute his thoughts had raced ahead of the ship to whatever lay waiting for them all on the other side of the ocean.

As he was about to step ashore in an imaginary New York

the hatch covering above was thrown open and all his thoughts were scattered. He shifted over to where he could see what was going on.

Down the ladder into the hold, one by one, and moving as though they were afraid, came a file of men and women. All of them were dressed in black, and the bundles which several of the women carried, Robert noticed, gave a sinister look to the humpback shadows thrown by the lamplight.

The bosun came down soon after them into the hold. On his orders the bondsmen were awakened and the hold was rearranged. Into Robert's bunk came a sleepy Newt and the man who had cursed them both on the first night in the cellar. The noise of people changing about and unpacking settled down in a while, but Robert, now cramped against the side of the ship, found it difficult to sleep for a long time after this.

Apart from crowding them together, the newcomers brought about other changes in the life in the hold. There was one thing that surprised Robert: Some of those who had been with them in the cellar in Liverpool and who had not said a kind word to Robert or the Newt before this now came looking for their support against those they called "the Rapparees," who, they said, were "turning their hold into a pigsty, unfit for decent people."

Robert and Newt kept as much as possible to themselves, but the atmosphere now was charged with violence. Though they pretended to ignore it, they were both sure that there would soon be a fight between the first inhabitants and those who had come aboard at Cork.

Something quite unexpected was to prevent this, however.

Several hours after Robert and the Newt had talked themselves to sleep, telling each other of their lives before they came to be aboard *The Charming Betty,* Robert awoke to hear the sound of crying.

It came from behind the curtain of rag which now divided the hold into the men's and women's quarters. As Robert listened it grew louder and from all over the hold came the noise of whispering.

Robert had thought the Newt was still asleep; he was surprised to find him wide awake, lying there and looking straight up at the slats of the bunk above.

"What is it, Newt?" he whispered. "What's happening now?"

The Newt did not seem to hear him. Robert felt awed by a completely different Newt from the one who had been chattering as usual several hundred words to the minute only a few hours before.

Robert kept silent for a while. "What are you thinking about, Newt?" he whispered again some time later.

"The fever," the Newt said without even turning to look at Robert. "If it's the fever I've seen it before in prisons." He sounded very old at that moment and very far away, as though he had drawn in entirely on himself.

There was a second change, a new and much more sinister atmosphere, in the hold now.

For one thing, they were left to themselves. The visits of the sailors became rare and brief. There were no mornings on deck to break the monotony and to divide day from night. There seemed to be no feeling of time passing, though the ship moved on; everything appeared to be suspended, so that it was difficult afterward to remember the proper order of the few things that did happen.

They left one another alone also; even Robert and the Newt lay hour after hour without speaking, listening to the creaking of the ship's timbers and the breathing about them. Each person in the quiet hold lay wide awake, waiting for the fever to go, as if hoping that by remaining quite still they would escape its notice.

At one time Robert forced himself out of this trancelike state to set off in search of a drink of water. He found the hatch open, and a group of sailors were carrying something awkwardly up the ladder. Robert looked up beyond them at the blue square of sky scattered with stars. A cool breeze seemed to come down from the world outside, shifting the heavy air in the hold where the fever was.

As he held his face up to the breeze, someone put his hand on Robert's shoulder. A sailor was trying to pass him to go up the ladder. The red wound, half healed, that ran from the man's chin right up to his hairline left Robert in no doubt at all that this was the sailor who had thrown himself overboard trying to escape.

Remembering that scene on the deck and the head held up to the lamp, he shuddered without meaning to. The sailor, noticing this and mistaking it for fear, said with a broad smile, "Don't worry yourself so; the Devil takes care of his chickens. You see, he'll see you safe for a hanging like your father before you." He winked, gripped Robert's arm, gave it a friendly squeeze, then went on his way up the ladder, whistling softly to himself as he went, as though he had no fear that night of the fever or of anything else.

Robert walked back to the bunk thinking of him. There was a sound of sobbing once more behind the curtain of rag. A second lantern, probably resting on the floor, threw a vivid orange glare with a brown edge onto the material as though the cloth were scorching. Robert felt his way carefully back into his own bunk.

It might have been an hour later, or a day later, when he woke to hear the Newt's voice. The Newt was talking in the same breathless manner he had used that first night in the cellar. But this time, instead of whispering, he spoke in a voice that sounded outrageously loud.

All the time he was staring straight up, his eyes wide open. Emotions seemed to flicker across his face as quickly as though they changed with each word he spoke. He smiled, pulled the corners of his mouth down, raised his eyebrows up, lowered them, grimaced. "We shall work seven years, Kestrel, Kestrel," the Newt said, catching up his breath to go on. "Seven, no more to be sure. And then we are to have a golden guinea if we are good and have worked with a will. Then we may do as we choose and see great ships and sail on them. We may save and be rich ourselves to own a carriage, Kestrel, a carriage and servants, and there are green fields and rich food to be had in America, America, and we may sleep, each of us, in a feather bed and have linen at table and cider, they say, and sweet pork even the poorest . . . !"

"Newt!" Robert called out to him. "Newt!"

Someone pulled at Robert's foot from the other side of the bunk, then dragged him over the Newt's body. A lantern was held up. In the glaring light he could see the bosun and the sailor with the red wound on the side of his face. Behind him all the time the Newt's voice seemed to get louder and louder. He felt something burning in his throat and chest and asked for a drink. The sailor held up a measure and poured the water into his mouth, but it cooled him for only a moment; and now it seemed to him they were trying to burn him with the lantern. He tried to get away from it and back to the bunk to see the Newt, but someone took him up and carried him. They put him down in a dark place and laid a damp cloth across his forehead.

He was dreaming now, going back on a series of confused journeys. Once he was standing by the lake with the Bird-taker and Ben. He tried to cool himself by taking up hand-fuls of snow and rubbing it against his burning skin. In another dream he was being pursued down the gorge. He escaped at last and rode his pony at full gallop into the countyard of the Hall—only to find that there, waiting for him in the doorway, was Captain Mask with a boathook in his hands.

For a long time there seemed to be little difference be-tween his sleep in which one nightmare followed another, and the periods of lying half awake and fitful, burning with the fever. Gradually he came to realize that he was being watched over and fed by the sailor with the face wound and by a woman.

Once, when he had been dreaming of the boat, he woke up, found himself alone and called out for the Newt. Then the sailor came quickly, took him firmly by the shoulders and pressed him back into the straw. "Hush now, will you." he ordered. "It's no time to go yelling your head off. Go back to sleep." But because Robert went on repeating the Newt's name over and over, he said almost harshly. "Be quiet. You've no call on him, neither you nor I, nor any of us."

"Oh Newt!" Robert said, now quietly. "Oh Newt!"

"Will you listen to me," the sailor said, pressing Robert's shoulders so hard with his thumbs that they began to ache. "You'll be leaving us yourself unless you're careful, do you understand me?" Robert nodded. "Do you want to get well?"

"Yes," Robert said.

"Well, you will if you choose," the sailor said, "but don't go and break yourself thinking about your friend. If you make a fight for it I'll help you. Hannah and I'll bring you your food. The two of us'll see you safe to America, be sure of it. . . . Have you good things to remember?" he asked.

Robert nodded.

"Then think on them. Think hard on them. Remember every good day you've ever had. And remember what it is you'll want to do when you're older. . . . Will you sleep?"

"I'll sleep," Robert said.

About a week later he managed to walk a few steps. His head felt clear; he seemed to have a new strength. "I can stand!" he called out to the woman he had come to call Hannah as he saw her walking toward him.

It was from Hannah that Robert learned what had happened during the weeks he had been ill and the part the sailor, Massey, had played.

"It was him that saved us, you and me, Jack, and others as

well," Hannah said in a voice so soft Robert could hardly hear her. "It was him, sure enough, bringing us what we needed at all hours, fighting the sickness like he had an army against him. He's a blessed soul, though he curses so terrible."

Massey himself would hear no word about the period of the fever. He watched Robert carefully, too, for those periods when a sudden wave of desolation would show itself on Robert's face and the loss of his friend would come to him, more overwhelming than anything he had known in his life before.

On one such moment he said, "We're but a day out of New York, the Mate tells me. If it's true, all I can say is I hope no bright-eyed Yankee-doodle spots our fever marks till we're sitting, you and me, Jack, with our boots under a table in one of the taverns of New York. I've known a ship before now turned out of Liverpool Roads with a shot fired across her bows from a man-o'-war, and all because she carried one man with fever from the Indies."

"But, Massey, they *must* let us ashore!" Robert said.

The sailor gave him a wry smile. "I'd say we'd *better* get ashore soon, for the larder's bare. There's not a plank of meat aboard, not a splinter of salt fish. As for the ship's biscuit, why, look here!"

He broke off a wedge of biscuit and rubbed it in his hands, then showed it around. Gray weevils had left the crumbs and were running around his palm. "They look spry enough on it, perhaps we'll find it passable." He gave a mischievous chuckle. "Right now they say it's a Lord Mayor's dinner up in the forecastle if they sit down to eat two front legs of a weevil at a sitting."

"Ah, shame, shame on you!" Hannah said, laughing.

"It's a cruel, hard world for a weevil, same as the rest of us," Massey pronounced solemnly. "Here's a pair of them running along together." He held his finger straight out as a ramp for the weevils to run on, then drew his hand closer to the lamplight so that Hannah and Robert could see. "Now here's an interfering old busybody coming to break them up. He's done it and off they go separately.

"I'll tell you a story about them—the three weevils," Massey said. "This one, do you see him?" Robert nodded. "Now he was a hard-working fellow if you like, an industrious silversmith's apprentice, skilled with his fingers. He could twist hot silver into barley twists, into roses and griffins for your candelabras and candlesticks and fashion little ladies' rings and patch boxes or snuff boxes for the gentlemen, all with delicate clasps and hinges. He had but one year to go until he became a craftsman, able to open his own shop and become rich.

"This beautiful weevil here—" Massey held it on the tip of his fingernail—"was the proud daughter of a slaver, a rich merchant with three ships, each out of Liverpool, taking blackamoors to the Indies from Guinea and bringing back tobacco, rum, sugar and molasses. Here he is, the father, very fat and jowelly, flourishing a big black walking stick with a silver bauble to top it, which he, the silversmith-weevil, remembers having made the very first time he claps eyes on the slaver. But this youngish weevil, the silversmith's apprentice, has been off to church early one Sunday morning, and there for the first time, he has seen milady, the slaver's daughter, this beautiful weevil here—isn't she lovely! He bows as he comes out of church; he makes a leg—so. He has been looking at her around pillars and over the ladies' powdered hair all through the service. Does she acknowledge him? She does! She even smiles, a very beautiful smile. Poor beau weevil! From Sunday to Sunday he does nothing but think of her; no sleep to speak of, no joy in his drinking, no pleasure in his bad companions. . . . Sunday, back he comes to the church. But she is not to be seen—disaster! Then, in his own master's shop early on the Monday morning, in from the street comes the beautiful miss slaver-weevil to have a salt cellar repaired. So she says. But he is a vain enough fellow to believe that she has actually found out where he works and has come along herself to take a look at him. But, to be short, they whisper, talk, promise to meet, meet, kiss, promise to meet again, do so—and so on and so on.

"Now the slaver-weevil hears about all these goings-on from some busybody, taps his daughter's confidence and summons the silversmith-weevil to his house; storms, rants and rages, and finally threatens him to be off and never come back. 'A silversmith's apprentice! Pah! What's this I hear? An impudent, upstart silversmith's apprentice making advances to *my* daughter—out, sah!' And he raps him soundly with the bauble the poor silversmith has made himself.

"Is the silversmith-weevil overawed by this? Not at all! But the more in love for the beating? I fear so. And the lady has learned her lesson so badly from the sound scolding she has had that she runs from the slaver's house to see the apprentice, not once, but five times within the calendar year.

"But then, when they plan to run away and marry in some other town, to leave on the very day the apprentice is to finish his apprenticeship and to be made a craftsman by the guild, the slaver, somehow, finds out their plan and makes one of his own. He goes—here he is, too, on his way—to find a friend, a sea captain, who used to be one of the slaver's own captains, a man whose face was torn by an African chief with no great wish to go in chains to the Indies and who now wears another skin over his own. This same man, when he hears of his friend's troubles, says to the slaver 'Enough, sir. Have no more fear. I leave in a week and your worries are over. I'll take this lad as crew for me on my ship, *The Charming Betty.*' 'But what,' says the slaver, 'if he be unwilling to go?' 'Why, no trouble at all, sir,' says this captain-friend. 'I've a gang of good men handy who will persuade this spirited beau to board our ship. Once aboard, we are bound for New York, and your daughter may marry an Earl!'

"And so," said Massey, "they did." And he crushed the

weevils one, two, three, with the heel of his hand and looked up with the same smile as before.

"Oh, Massey!" Robert said.

"Ahoy! Sailor below!" came a cry down into the hold as soon as the hatch was flung open.

Massey got up and walked to the ladder. "Aye?" he shouted back.

"Land ho!" said the voice from the deck. "Come aloft and report to the Captain how many below can walk ashore."

"Aye," Massey called. "Land, eh?" he said to Robert and Hannah. "Pray Heaven they send out a port captain that doesn't know fever!"

✑ 6 ✑

Landfall and Sold Again

IT WAS a bitterly cold December afternoon when *The Charming Betty* came sailing into New York harbor. A small group of bondservants, the four men, two women and a boy who had survived the fever huddled together and gazed across a gray sea at the land. They had passed a series of flat, uninhabited islands and now the ship was bearing down quickly on a promontory and a sizable town.

There's a spire, Robert thought! They have churches like ours, ships like this one. But he was a little disappointed. He wondered sadly what the Newt would have made of all this. Had they come so far to find these gray hills, this gray winter sea, this very ordinary-looking town at the end of their voyage?

But it was not long before they could see the town in detail, and then Robert's interest returned. The dock was not unlike the one in Liverpool. Behind it, however, there were rows of buildings, some as large as barns with great double doors, others with stepped fronts in the Dutch style and bright-red roofs. Everything looked trim and prosperous, if a little severe in the winter sunlight.

They appeared to be moving rapidly enough, yet the land kept its distance. Then the ship turned, the sailors scattered and swarmed the yards, the canvas was drawn up, the dock hurried to meet them, the ropes went out and were made fast ashore, the boat slowed and came to a stop beside the wharf. The long voyage was over.

The bondservants were to be landed immediately, before any rumor of the fever passed to the shore. As soon as the gangplank was in place, therefore, the bosun approached them with a party of sailors to escort them to the town.

In the confusion of leaving the ship Robert caught sight of Massey. He had joined the group of bondservants at the back. He was standing close to Hannah, carrying her bundle high on his shoulder so that it covered half his face, and he wore a plain canvas jacket over his own. Robert was about to go back to speak to him when some instinct cautioned him to keep his place at the front and not call attention to his friend.

In a moment the party set off. They left the deck and walked single file down the plank to the dock. The gangplank seemed dangerously springy to Robert, and after two or three steps on land he stumbled. The ground gave him a strange feeling after the weeks at sea; he felt dizzy, as though the fever had come back.

They spent no time on the dock before being marched off, a file of sailors walking on either side of the column of bondservants, so that any inquisitive colonist would have suspected that a party of desperate criminals was being brought ashore, instead of the wretched group of survivors they were. Robert could see almost nothing of where they were going and, anyway, at that moment he felt so ill he had to concentrate all his attention on keeping up. He never noticed that Hannah had tried twice to come up the column to speak to him but had been ordered back each time to her place. At the very moment while his two friends were anxiously trying to decide what risks they could take to help him without trapping themselves, Robert was quite lost to everything but the fear that he might faint in the street.

How far they had gone he had no idea when the bondsmen were led up a flight of steps into a large, dark hall and told they could stretch out on the floor there and rest. He had just settled himself down, exhausted, when he was dragged to his feet once more by the bosun.

"Come, where's your friend—eh?" the man shouted almost in his face. "That man Massey and the girl—where did they go? Speak up, or I'll shake it out of you." He shook Robert hard this way and that, but soon realized from his expression that he would learn nothing and flung him to the floor again.

"Good for Massey, I say," one of the sailors jeered when the bosun had gone, taking half the escort with him. "Cut off clean with the girl. What chance of their hooking him out of this town?"

"No odds at all," another said and they laughed.

But Robert, however tired and weak he might feel, lay wide awake now, realizing that the others had left him. His sense of disappointment struggled inside him with the knowledge that they had every right to escape when they could. He ought to have been glad they had got away, but all he could think of was that he was now as friendless as he had been that first hour in the cellar in Liverpool. This time there would be no Newt to lift his spirits. The new loss of friends seemed added to the other, so recent still, and still quite unhealed. Massey and Hannah had helped to try to comfort him over the Newt's death, and now they had left him as though they cared nothing for him!

Gradually he got the better of his self-pity. It was his own fault, after all, that he had been left behind; he was too weak to run. He would have to gain what strength he could and look for his own opportunities. If Massey and Hannah were still in New York he would join them somehow. And so when a meal was brought that night, the first meal of any substance the bondservants had seen for many weeks, Robert ate more than he wanted and then lay down to sleep, putting all sad thoughts resolutely out of his head.

On the following morning the rumor started that an auction of the bondsmen was to take place immediately, again before the news of the fever became generally known and prevented the sale. As if to confirm the rumor, Captain Mask arrived early in the day to inspect what was left of his stock. He looked at each of the survivors in turn, his expression becoming graver by the minute. In the end he came to Robert.

"You've cost me too much, Jack, and now I see you're no prize. What shall we do with you?" The Captain moistened his lips, considering the matter. "Either I sell you this morning for good Colonial money or . . . or it's back you come with me on *The Charming Betty*." He drew closer, so that Robert could see his strange, freakish face all too clearly. "I give you fair warning, Jack, if that's to be so, I'll work whatever value's left out of you. Remember what I say. If I should bring some colonist over to show you off, look chipper —do you hear?—look spry! Aye, and if he wants a word with you, make yourself out a farmer's boy, a hand at herding cattle or what you will. I say this," he whispered closely, "mention one word of the fever and back we go, Jack, you and I, till we part for good—eh?" Robert nodded. "I've no liking for you, Jack," Captain Mask said, "no liking for you at all, and I aim to be rid of you one way or the other!" He spun quickly about on his heel and walked off.

Soon after he left, the hall was tidied by a sweeper, and a clerk came in and spread his papers out at a desk in the corner. The bosun and the three sailors on duty lined the bondservants up with their backs against one wall under the fall of light through high windows. Here they waited in silence for what seemed like an hour or more.

At last the doors were thrown open and Captain Mask returned. Into the hall behind him came a crowd of twenty or more men, dressed in the clothes of a dozen trades and professions. These, jostling one another for place as they hurried forward to see what was offered, were the buyers. They went from one bondservant to the next with the Captain or the bosun usually at their elbow.

A sour-looking fellow dressed in baggy, home-made clothes and with a broad face covered with warts came shambling over and stood studying Robert. He motioned Robert to take off his coat. Remembering his instructions to do what he was told and to make himself generally helpful, Robert started to pull off the coat when he felt Captain Mask's fingers close hard on his wrist.

"He's a strong boy," Captain Mask said to the colonist, "son of a Dorset farmer. Though he's a trifling cold at the moment, sir, as you see, he's a strong lad and can turn a ewe on its back at shearing. He'll work with a will."

The stranger looked his fill at Robert and pouted. It was obvious the Captain's words had put him off-balance. "Aye, maybe, maybe," he muttered and walked off.

"Keep your coat on, you idiot!" snarled the Captain when he had gone, "and rub some blood up into your face!"

If Robert could have sold himself to anyone in the room at that moment he would have done it gladly. He rubbed his cheeks, held himself straight and showed what he hoped was a forthright expression. Underneath, he felt sick and dispirited. He hated the dusty hall and these people prodding and prying. He felt he might well have been something shoddy offered for sale, like a lame animal in a pen on market day at Bower. It was worse to have to play up to this situation himself. But at the back of his mind there was only one thought—the prospect of another journey under the Captain.

He looked about among the two dozen buyers for the best of them. Their expressions ranged from stupid and greedy to sharp and greedy. Not one of them had a friendly face, and not one of them now showed the slightest interest in Robert.

He was beginning to despair when he saw the poorly dressed sweeper who had cleaned out the hall before the auction started. This man made his way through the buyers and stood a little way from Robert, looking him over closely from head to foot.

Surely, Robert thought, *he's* not going to bid for me! The man was in worse rags than he was himself.

After assuring himself, however, the sweeper siddled up close to Robert and thrust something into his hand. Robert knew by the feel that it was a square of folded paper. He put it quickly into his pocket, without looking down, and thanked the sweeper. The message delivered, the other man was off again, lost in the crowd. There was no opportunity to read the note without being noticed, but even the touch of it in his pocket brought all Robert's hope flooding back: Massey had found a way of reaching him!

At that very moment a sprightly little man, with a red face and patched brown coat from which a red polka-dot handkerchief exploded at the breast pocket, strode quickly into the room, took a chair, turned it about, climbed on and clapped his hands, shouting out, "Order! Order!" As soon as he had silence and the room's attention, he took off his glasses and polished them with the handkerchief.

"Gentlemen," he called out briskly, "you have had ample opportunity to satisfy yourselves. Pray come now and bid.

"The service, as you know, of each person here on view is to be sold for the period of seven years from this day in bondage to the purchaser by the Captain here in payment to him of the passage of these persons. At the end of seven years you are yourselves bound by these papers to release the said person, a free man or woman.

"Very well, I will take Joseph Simons, ironworker, first. Bring him up! Gentlemen, start your bidding. I will take no less than a hundred to start us . . ."

The bidding was brisk and the auctioneer hard put to it to follow. The sale was made and Joseph Simons (the man who had threatened Robert and the Newt in the cellar and who had shared their bunk on the boat) was bonded for seven years' service. The papers were signed and the man left with two of the buyers.

One by one the men were auctioned and then the remaining woman was put up. Here the bidding lagged more than once. Each time it did so, the auctioneer would take off his glasses and begin polishing them. "Come, come, gentlemen," he admonished three times over, "let's not keep a lady waiting." And three times over there was an appreciative chuckle around the hall.

Finally they came to the last item on the list, one Jack Allen, a farmer's boy from Dorset. The auctioneer read this and then looked at Robert with an expression of outright disbelief. He took off his spectacles, polished them furiously for the twentieth time and replaced them on his red nose. "What am I bid, gentlemen?"

Robert noticed that there were now no more than a dozen people in the hall and not one of them answered the appeal.

"Come, friends, let me have your price. I start you at forty guineas."

"At fifty!" Captain Mask corrected him.

The auctioneer looked across at the Captain over the rim of his spectacles, then gazed down at Robert, pulled out his handkerchief and blew hard and long. "At fifty guineas," he amended himself with dignity, then waited. There was an almost complete silence in the room. Nearly a minute passed.

"Come make your bids, friends." (The auctioneer sounded peevish now. He looked at the Captain as though asking him if they needed to go on with this.) "The lad's a trifle under the weather, I grant you, from the sea air and the ship's biscuit, but you have a bargain here in disguise." There was a loud guffaw from the crowd.

"I bid you twenty-eight *pounds*—no more, not sixpence!" said a voice. Robert saw it was the broad-faced farmer who had spoken.

"Have I any advance—" the auctioneer began.

"Have done!" Captain Mask interrupted. "Twenty-eight's sufficient. Come, Jack," he ordered, "put your mark to these papers."

Robert took the quill and was about to write his name

where the long yellow finger of the clerk was pointing when he heard the Captain's voice again at his ear, whispering "Your mark, Jack, your mark!"

Robert drew a great X. The clerk wrote under it "Mark of the boy, Jack Allen," then passed the paper across to the farmer, who read it laboriously through and, afterward, wrote beneath Robert's X in great black capitals CALVIN MOORE.

"Come then, sir, your money and the boy is yours," the clerk said. The stranger dug deep into a pocket and brought out a leather purse and a wad of soiled paper. "I'll give you coin for twenty and script for the rest," he said. He counted the twenty and passed it with a note across to the Captain. Captain Mask folded his arms and looked down on it. "Take no offense, sir, but I trust no colonist farmers to pay me their paper, their dollars, eights or dabloons. Have you eight English pounds more, then we are trim?"

"My credit is good in this town," the farmer muttered.

"I've no reason to doubt that, sir; but as my information is that you intend to be out of New York immediately, I've no choice but to ask you for the coin."

The farmer hesitated, then counted out eight pounds in small coins and pushed these over the table, his face now sourer and blacker than ever. The clerk tapped the coins one after another with the point of his quill, looked up and gave a nod to the Captain. The farmer took up the deed and crushed it into his pocket.

"Have no fear, Mr. Moore, you have a good lad there," Captain Mask said with something of a sneer. He scooped up the coins and put them away in his waistcoat with the usual precise movement. "A good boy, sir," he repeated, "a worker."

"Get your possessions, lad," the farmer said, turning away from the officer. When Robert told him he had none, the man blinked at him incredulously. "Not a shirt?" Robert shook his head.

The farmer took him by the sleeves and pulled him close. "Then listen, Jack, George, John, or whatever your name may be," he said. "You owe me twenty-eight pounds in sterling. That's one for every quarter-day of your service . . . and the food you eat . . . and what we put on your back!" He had screwed up his face in rage so tightly his eyes were lost in the folds of flesh. "Money's hard come by in this land you've chosen to come to—hard! Hard!" he said. "You'll work to pay me, sixteen hours to the day for seven years, not a day less . . . and speak civil—aye?"

Robert nodded. "Yes, sir."

"Sir me no 'sirs'!" the farmer rasped. "I'm none of your lords of Old England! Call me Mr. Moore, but speak no more than you must."

But Robert had heard only half of the tirade. He had been watching Captain Mask walk away down the hall, a hall empty now except for the clerk gathering papers and a knot of sailors. "I'll see him no more," he whispered to the retreating figure, and it was almost with joy that he followed his new master from the building.

Outside the streets were crowded and busy. There was snow on the ground that had not been there the day before. The people looked well dressed and prosperous. A group of girls went past, their cloaks trimmed with fur. Another girl passed them carrying a basket from which dangled the heads of a pair of geese. In the crowd Robert noticed a group of Quakers, a peddler in motley, and several red-coated soldiers. A vendor of roast chestnuts had set up his brazier at a corner, and the smell of the roasting nuts came unkindly clear in the air to Robert, reminding him with a sudden pang of unhappiness how long it had been since he had been cut off from enjoying such things.

He found an opportunity as they walked among the crowd to draw the note from his pocket. Squinting down, he read the message in his cupped hand. "Kestrel," it said on the outside, and, inside: "Be at the Nut Brown Maid, an inn hard by the Bowling Green and before the steeple of Trinity Church, at six o'clock this evening. The place lies not two hundred yards due west of where you are now. I will be dressed in a gray coat and will stand by the fire with my back to the room from six until half past to wait your coming. I dare not stay longer. Another is with me and misses you. If you are prevented tonight, do not lose hope. Your friends will watch for you and succeed in reaching you at a better opportunity. Good luck. Yr. Hon'd friend—Weevil."

"Why do you stare so at your feet?" Calvin said, cuffing his shoulder. "Are you wooden-headed then, as well? Stay close to me."

When he looked up, Robert noticed that they were passing an iron railing. Behind this was a patch of ground scattered with gravestones and vaults. Beyond was a church with a high steeple. A hundred yards farther on, Robert and Calvin passed under a frame of scaffolding, climbed some stairs and entered a doorway.

They were no sooner inside than Robert began to suspect that Calvin had led him straight to the Nut Brown Maid.

It was an inn for certain and an inn close to a church. He was standing in the entrance of a large room, a cheerful place, with a great fire of logs burning at the far end. Although it was two in the afternoon at the latest, he searched at once for a man in a gray coat, standing with his back to the room. Instead, four officers, all in scarlet, were sprawled on the benches of the fire nook, their legs thrust out in front of them, all four apparently asleep.

The room was crowded with people, both standing in the center and sitting in the booths at either side. Smoke came up from the long-stemmed clay pipes, while from a series of pewter punch bowls set on an oak table in the room's center clouds of steam were rising. Two women with mob caps on their heads, one of them a Negress, were hurrying to and fro about the room with tankards and trays of pewter cups.

"Keep close," Calvin said, "and don't gape."

But Robert had fixed his attention on the Negro servant. He had never seen anyone before with a dark skin. He knew she must be a slave; probably she had come to America as he had come, locked in the hold of a ship—yet she had been brought all the way not from Europe but from a mysterious Africa. The girl, mistaking the reason for Robert's attention, and taking in at a glance his clothes and his pale face, chose a minute when Calvin had gone into one of the booths to speak with someone. Then she came over to him and put one of the pewter cups full of hot, spiced rum punch into his hands with a lump of white bread, also warm and seasoned with cinnamon and sultanas. Robert took these, a little confused by this sudden kindness, and thanked her. "Merry Christmas!" she wished him, smiled, then hurried on her way.

Christmas! Robert thought. He lifted the little pewter cup and sucked the rum slowly in. It went down warm all the way into his empty stomach. Then he bit off a piece of the bread and swallowed. Christmas! He closed his eyes and immediately a picture of the Hall came into his mind, the roast goose on the table, the puddings and holiday cakes—a picture so vivid he seemed to be back there for a minute.

He opened his eyes, and he was not.

Two men walked past Robert, glanced around him into the booth, then went into another close by and sat down. Calvin was too engrossed in his conversation to notice the glances the newcomers gave him, but Robert saw from their expressions that they must know Calvin well.

"Calvin Moore in New York?" the first one said loud enough for Robert to hear. "Ha," the other chuckled, "he's a new wife to please." He called out for drink, and Robert's friend, the Negress, came hurrying over. Robert shifted his position so that he could hear their remarks about his new master. "Did that girl Mary die, then?" the second man asked.

"She did. They say the life wore her out and I don't wonder. The farm's all stone I've seen it."

"Who did he marry?"

"There's the plum," said his informant gleefully. "He married Agatha, old Matthew Hellfire-and-Brimstone's eldest daughter—do you know her?"

"I do not," the second man admitted.

"Then you've missed something. Aye, he's a rare one for courage, is Calvin. Come drink to him! Give the fellow his due. There's a wife that could drive a man to Hell for the comfort of a quiet fire."

They brought up their tankards and drank. "She held out on him, mind you," said the first speaker after a pause. "Made him promise to get her a servant before she'd venture to keep house with him. Likely she knew how Mary went."

"Calvin's a hard man," the second speaker observed.

"Aye, Calvin Moore's hard enough, but she's a match for him. I wager you she'll outlast him, will old Matthew's oldest shrew. They've their tongues and their tricks from the witches of Salem, have that tribe of women.

Robert listened hard but he could catch no more of what they were saying. A third man joined them in the booth, a tall, thin person in black, wearing a periwig. They made room for him and shouted for more drink.

The Negress came again, bringing another tankard. She stayed to speak to Robert and took the cup from him. He asked her if this was the Nut Brown Maid and she told him it was indeed. But she had seen no one of Massey's description when Robert gave it. She agreed, however, to give him the message that Robert had been there and that he would do his best to meet his friend at six that evening.

Their conversation was cut short when Calvin came out of the booth. The man he had been speaking with came after him still talking. Robert heard him say to Calvin, "Calvin, I'd give you more, willingly, believe me but I've the holiday to think of. I've my own family and trade's poor enough. You surely have enough to buy provisions."

"I've the ten dollars in script you've given me, no more,

Lucius, but I thank you for that," Calvin Moore growled in reply. He drew on his brown overcoat.

The other man stood hesitating. "Very well, a good Christmas, Calvin, and God keep you," he said.

"Come, boy!" Calvin called out abruptly.

They were about to walk away when Calvin saw the two men Robert had overheard discussing him in the next booth. Calvin nodded gravely to them. When he caught sight of the man in the periwig, however, his expression changed. He turned his head sharply away, drew up the collar of his coat and hurried from the inn with Robert behind him.

Not far from the Nut Brown Maid, in a yard, stood a derelict-looking wagon that had once been painted blue. Tied to a tree were two emaciated horses, waiting to draw the wagon. As Calvin Moore and Robert crossed the yard a woman got down stiffly from the driving board to meet them.

"Not more than two hours I've been waiting for you!" she cried out in a harsh nasal screech. "Did you want me to freeze, Mr. Moore?"

She had a pinched, bony face, handsome in its way, Robert noticed, but marred where her heavy eyebrows met in a single black band, a scowl of rage Robert was to find more or less permanent. A mob cap sat on her unruly hair so insecurely it looked as though it would fall off as she shook with anger each time she spoke.

"Is this the boy?" she said, pointing.

"Aye," Calvin answered. "His name's Jack. He's a good worker, they assured me so."

"A good worker!" The woman snorted with contempt. "A bag of bones more likely! I knew well enough, Mr. Moore, I should have come with you to see for myself what sort of a scarecrow you would find me to keep up our bargain."

"You'd not have been allowed in, Agatha, as I told you," Calvin said.

The woman approached them, then suddenly leapt back,

her eyes flashing. "Drink," she screeched. "You've been drinking, is it, while I wait in the cold?"

"Peace! Great heavens, I've had none," Calvin protested.

"The boy, then." She came close and sniffed at Robert's mouth. "It is!" she cried in triumph and she fell upon Robert with both hands, cuffing him about the head. "You choose well," she called out between blows: "a drunkard and no more than a boy! You choose well, Mr. Moore, when you choose your wife's servants!"

Calvin pinned Robert by the arms and dragged him out of her range. "Get up in the back, you." And he added a kick of his own to his wife's cuffs.

Robert started off, his ears tingling with the blows. But instead of climbing up into the cart, he went around to the back, put the wagon between himself and his assailants and then sprinted away for all he was worth.

"Stop thief—stop!" Calvin shouted. Someone took up the cry. They sounded very close. Robert clenched his fists, put his head down and ran harder still.

A turning led from the yard. Robert slid on the soft snow, cut the corner close and pelted on down another lane. Not very far ahead he saw the spire of a church. If he could shake off the pursuit and hide near the church, he thought, he would be safe—free for good!

Just at this moment a man came walking out of a doorway, unsuspecting, and collided with Robert. As he fell, he caught at Robert's coat to hold himself up. Robert swung away and almost broke free, but the man clutched wildly again and his arm struck Robert in the face, knocking him down.

Calvin had him dragged up onto his feet. A dog snapped at his heels and hostile faces met his look on every side. His face was numb, his nose bled. His lungs heaved after the run. He had put all his strength into escaping and now he could hardly walk. When he coughed it racked his chest. What annoyed him most was that his eyes were streaming with the blow as though he were crying!

"A fine boy you bought me," Agatha said. "Did you beat him for running off?"

"Aye," Calvin answered, "he's beaten. Let's be off." He dragged Robert to the back and half boosted, half flung him in. Then he took off his belt and strapped his legs together. Afterward he tied Robert's hands, threw a blanket over him and left him, trussed up, staring at the sky, his chest still heaving.

Robert heard Calvin secure the horses, climb up onto the front of the wagon and they started off.

He tried his hands, but they were firmly tied. He could move about a little, but not enough to roll off the wagon. All his immediate chance of escape seemed to have gone. After a while he noticed that there were no more buildings to be seen, only a few bare branches; probably they were out of the town already.

As soon as his breath came back, however, Robert began to feel quite light-headed, almost gay. He had shown them! "Bag of bones!" Shown them a good pair of heels—that stupid auctioneer, the man who had guffawed during the auction, Captain Mask, Ben, the Birdtaker—the whole lot of them. If it hadn't been for one bit of bad luck he'd have been away by now—free, free as air, free as the people in the streets, free as he had been once, ages ago it seemed, in England—and free for all their efforts to stop him.

He had been caught. Massey would come that night to the inn and here he would be, trussed up and helpless in the back of a wagon somewhere on the road out of New York. But they could tie him up, chain him, do what they liked, he knew for the first time it was only a question of waiting; the opportunity would come and he was ready for it. He would get back now, whatever happened. He tucked his head down and brushed off the dried blood from his nose on the blanket. When he looked up into the sky again he grinned wickedly.

✑ 7 ✑

The New England Farmer

LATE AT NIGHT several days after Christmas, Agatha and Robert arrived at Calvin Moore's farm.

A more desolate scene would be difficult to imagine. Snow lay gray and deep under a veiled moon. A great brake of pine trees towered like a threatening wave over the one man-made thing in sight—a low building with two windows, showing no welcoming light. A bitterly cold wind was blowing, bringing up powdered snow from the drifts.

The farmhouse itself proved to be no more than a cabin, built one wall of stone and three of logs and mud. It had two small rooms below and a loft under the roof. Against the cabin on one side leaned a low stone barn, which seemed to crumble off at the far end in a clutter of wooden coops and outhouses. Inside the cabin there were fewer and poorer furnishings than Robert had ever seen in a house; the meanest laborer at Tice Hall had more possessions than this in his cottage.

In Calvin's absence the farm had been left in the care of a younger brother. After repeated knocking the brother appeared at the door, a patchwork quilt about his shoulders, to curse them roundly for arriving back in the middle of the night. A violent argument began at once between the brother and Agatha which lasted until noon on the following day when the young man rode away.

Robert was never to forget that first night. There was no fire to be had, and the inside of the cabin was as cold, as the outside. After several days traveling on the road, Robert had become used to the permanent ache of cold, but in the endless delay—unhitching the horses, bedding them down in the barn and bringing in the provisions and stores to the cabin—Robert suffered new and worse pains in his fingers and toes. Finally everything was settled and he was shown where to sleep—a patch of the floor in the kitchen covered with corn husks.

The following morning he was aroused long before first light. Using the flint-and-tinder box, he lit the fire, then scoured pots, helped Calvin in the barn with the animals, drew water from the creek through a hole in the ice, dragged in wood and split kindling, cleared snow, mended one of the window frames with a fresh sheet of parchment, and otherwise fetched and carried until he fell asleep again on the floor of the kitchen at about eight that night and the day was over.

After this, one winter's day followed another of the same unrelieved drudgery. When the heavy snows came it meant that all three of them were confined together in the small house. When this happened there was no escape from the sound of Agatha's voice and from her scolding and bullying except in the barn, which was attached to the house by a passageway. The barn was always cold, drafty and wet underneath with crushed snow and mud. It was cramped, too, with Calvin's stock of two horses, two cows and three goats, crowded in with ducks and chickens. But there was always something useful to do here to keep the animals alive through the hard American winter. Robert grew skillful in looking after them, and he felt proud of his skill. Above all, he could keep his own company there, away from his master and his master's wife.

One morning in January Robert woke with the feeling that there was something very different about the atmosphere in the cabin. It worried him that he could not tell what this was right away. He lit the fire and the flames gave some light to see by. Nothing looked different, and yet it *felt* quite different.

He tried the door. Nothing would open it outward, though it was unlocked and he had put his whole weight against it. More mystified still, he took out the frame that was covered with parchment and which served as one of the windows. When he did this, Robert found himself looking at a solid wall of snow, blocking the window from the sill to the top.

He called to Calvin, who came down to look. They pushed and packed the snow back, making the beginning of a tunnel, and then climbed over the sill into the hole. After this they enlarged the hole in the same way, but still there was no sign of the outside world! Then, unexpectedly, by thrusting his arm up, Robert broke through above. A small avalanche of snow fell down into the space they had cleared. They packed this against the walls and tried to build steps of packed snow to the surface, but the snow was soft and it crumbled under their feet.

Calvin brought out a pair of snowshoes which he had traded from the Indians during an earlier winter. These were roughly shaped, single lengths of ash that had been peeled, heated and looped around, then bound, one end to the other behind the loop with leather thongs. Across the loop itself other thongs had been crisscrossed, and in the middle a wooden block was secured to fit the instep of the wearer's feet. Calvin strapped the snowshoes to his boots and then, with Robert's help, climbed through to the surface and disappeared.

He was gone for little more than a minute, and when he

came down again he looked concerned. The drift had come to the top of the roof. If it thawed a little during the day and then froze hard, it might break the cabin apart, while the weight of the snow alone was enough to collapse the roof.

Calvin took off the snowshoes and gave them to Robert to put on. He told him to take the fire shovel and clear as much as he could while he himself went off to find the spade.

Robert scrambled to the top with difficulty and looked about. The chimneystack stood up, a comical black shape like a hat someone had left resting on the surface of the snow. A trail of gray smoke rose in a leisurely fashion to the dark gray sky from which snowflakes were still falling. The brake of pine trees also topped the snow, but they were dwarf trees now, no more than five or six feet high. Otherwise Robert could look for hundreds of yards in every direction and see nothing but the same unbroken white level.

If it had continued snowing hard Robert wondered whether they would all have been buried alive in the night while they slept. Down there beneath his feet at that very moment were two human beings, horses, goats, cows, and chickens. Up here there was not a sign of them except for the small space where he had broken through and for the rising smoke.

Robert stood for a moment gazing about in awe, and then, moved by a sudden impulse, he set to work, digging as though the very lives of those beneath him depended on it.

He cleared fast, throwing the snow as far as he could and enlarging the tunnel to the window. Calvin joined him, walking on huge bundles of straw and rag. It was not long before they had taken the weight of snow from the roof. After that they uncovered each wall, sloping the snow up gradually and packing the escarpments firmly to prevent a fall. This took the whole day, and at the end the cabin looked as though it sat in the middle of a great white saucer.

At about four that afternoon Robert was working alone finishing one side and standing on the edge of the snow parapet. It had become suddenly colder in the last minute or so, and Robert stopped work to look up. The sun was just touching the horizon. It was huge, a deep red, the color of a poppy, with something of the purple of a poppy around its edge. It took a long time to sink through the vapors of white mist and to disappear.

The instant the last trace of it had gone the sky began to darken. Within a few minutes the moon was shining clearly and it might have been the middle of the night. Piles of snow where Robert had been working, some of them with weird shapes like giants or like prehistoric animals, cast their shadows now in the moonlight. Robert stood there for a minute, leaning on the spade. The instant he had stopped work he had felt the piercing cold in the air. It would freeze hard that night. A wild barking started up from somewhere far away, so that he could just hear it—probably timber wolves. Robert wondered how they had escaped the smothering fall of snow. What a country this was! It seemed terrible to him that anything, however wild, should have to spend the night out there, and he went quickly himself to what shelter he had.

A great lethargy seemed to have settled on them all with the coming of the blizzard. It required an effort of will now to do even those jobs that had to be done to keep them alive, and as the weeks when they were shut in by snow dragged on, the time told, in different ways, on each of them. Agatha hardly spoke except to complain or to give Robert an order. Calvin used no more than a dozen words between dawn and dusk. Only once a week, on Sunday evening, was a candle sacrificed with something like ceremony in that house. Then for exactly an hour Calvin read aloud from the Bible. He read without expression, moving his thumb forward from word to word. When the candle had burned down to the measuring pin stuck in the wax, Calvin stopped reading, often in mid-sentence, and when he had snuffed out the candle they would find their way to bed as they usually did by the flickering light of the fire.

At the end of March, when most of the deep snow had thawed from the tracks, Calvin set off to ride to New York to buy seeds and provisions for the coming season. He rode alone, and in his absence he expected Robert to run the farm.

The days he was away seemed even harsher to Robert than the others. Without her husband to draw it on himself occasionally, Agatha's temper was directed entirely at Robert.

A week passed and Calvin rode in, with almost nothing— no seed, no provisions, except for one side of bacon, a sack of poor flour and a little salt.

That night there was no sleep to be had in the cabin. In the loft over Robert's head Agatha shouted at Calvin, her voice rising time and again to an eerie note, so maniac and inhuman Robert felt a strange horror grip him as he waited each time, knowing the note was about to come again. Below her voice he could hear Calvin snarling, until there was a hush, followed by the sound of violent blows being struck, then a further pause and the sound of sobbing, stifled, as though by a pillow. This sobbing went on for a long time. When it was quiet at last, Robert lay still wide awake. The crackling of the fire and the low wind outside appeared to have taken over the same argument, the same harsh tones as the voices. It was another hour before Robert slept.

For two days after that, neither Calvin nor Agatha would speak to each other. Whatever they needed to communicate was passed through Robert, who for his part was cuffed by one and snarled at by the other.

On the second day of this forced truce two men rode in to meet Calvin. They were the first visitors of the year, and the duties of hospitality were rigid in that isolated region; but these men stayed no more than an hour before starting back the way they had come. They left without even a meal.

Robert, who had not known of their arrival, met them as

they were leaving. He was driving in the two cows, from a
pasture he had found for them near the creek. The two
strangers reined up their horses for a minute to watch him.
There was something familiar about the taller of the two,
and Robert remembered clearly that he had seen him that
winter morning before Christmas in the Nut Brown Maid.
He was the man wearing the periwig who had made so
immediate and unfavorable an impression on Calvin as they
left the inn. Now he and his companion scrutinized Robert
and the two cows, whispered between themselves and then,
with no word of greeting, started off down the muddy lane.

When Robert came into the cabin, Agatha was standing in
the kitchen with her hands on her hips, looking at Calvin.
Papers lay strewn over the table in front of him.

"I can't pay," Calvin was saying to her. "How can I pay?"

"Then they'll take everything—everything, even the boy!"
Agatha said.

"There's no need of that," Calvin muttered to the floor.
"Those two will be gone for a week or more. When they
return they may have what I choose to leave them."

"Aye?" Agatha questioned, not understanding his
meaning.

"We'll go west into the wilderness . . ." Calvin began.

"No!" Agatha cried out. "You've a farm here, you've
something—"

"I've nothing, woman!" he interrupted her savagely and
he crashed the table with his fist. "Nothing but a building I
raised with my own hands and fields I cleared of rock. Now
for seed through the years to fill our bellies it's gone—gone to
the New Yorkers. Let them have it. *No!*" he shouted. "That
Tory lawyer shan't have it, nor that catchpenny merchant! As
I built it, so I'll burn it, all that will burn! We'll go
tonight." Calvin struck each word out on the table as he
spoke it, struggling with himself as though to talk so much
was hurting him.

Agatha watched him. "You know best, Mr. Moore," she

said at the end—the first such words Robert had ever heard from her. She spoke them in a voice quite unlike her own, as though she were unsure of herself, very much afraid. "The boy will pack the cart . . . ?"

"Aye, aye," Calvin said, dazed, as if her words meant nothing to him, still concentrating as he was on his own hard-wrought ideas. "We leave tonight!" he repeated and fixed his gaze past the other two now, staring through the open door. "We'll take the new road, the military road, and find rich lands, good lands as I hear in town, free, green and ready for growing, and no New York Tories crying 'Interest!' "

Agatha hesitated, started for the door, then stopped and turned back to face him. All the anger had drained from her face. She stood looking at Calvin without emotion. When she spoke her voice was flat and very quiet. "We'll find savages," she said. "We'll find more stone fields, forests no axe can clear, swamp fever and the wilderness grave, Mr. Moore.

"Come, boy," she said to Robert, speaking with no trace of harshness. "Come, don't stand idle. We've work to do if we leave tonight."

They went as they had arrived, by the light of a veiled moon, the wagon packed high, the cows and goats tethered behind. The sky glowed red and resounded with the crackle of burning logs. Calvin had killed all but four of the laying hens, a cockerel and a pair of ducks. He himself had carried the burning brand from the fire and shavings to light one spot after another. He had not allowed them to start off until he had seen the farm nearly burned out, until he had made certain that there was nothing left behind to cover a penny's worth of his debts to the New Yorkers. While the fire raged and crackled he had seemed almost gay. But as soon as he turned his back on the scene and started up the wagon, he slumped over the driving board, shut his eyes and would speak to no one.

8

The Wilderness Road

THEY FOUND, soon enough, that it was far too early in the year to be at the mercy of the weather on the road. Where deep snowdrifts had so recently melted, thick, gray mud made the track almost impassable, sucking at the wheels of the cart, at the horses' legs and at the feet of those who stumbled along beside the cart. Sometimes the wheels stuck fast in the quagmires. Then Calvin and Robert had to unload everything and carry it to firm ground so that the lightened cart could be pulled free. Once even this failed. Then they were two days in the same place trying to save the cart, working with mud to their waists, binding the wheels with branches, fixing ropes to the axle and to a makeshift windlass. When, at last, they had heaved, pulled and wound the cart out of the grip of the morass and up onto firmer ground, neither they nor the horses could go any farther. They slept that second night where they were, huddled together, humans and animals, with only the cart as a cover against the icy April rain. When they woke Robert found the two cows and a goat were dead.

The only thing that could be said for this terrible journey was that as the hardship increased it forced a sort of unspoken alliance upon the three of them. There were now no sarcastic words from Agatha: she hardly spoke at all. And no words came from Calvin (a grunt when the wagon stuck fast, a grunt when they freed it again). In the trial of their endurance there was no servant, no master; all three pitted what strength they possessed together, shivered together at night and ate what little they had in three equal portions.

In this way they spent a month in going little more than a hundred miles, to arrive one morning, three skeletons in mud-caked rags, walking beside a broken cart, two near-dead horses drawing it, and two goats behind, at a town of twenty ugly wooden cabins with the proud name of Dorchester.

There was, it was true, a main street to this town, stone-paving laid for a few hundred yards. Robert, his head down, still straining at the cart like a galley slave at his oar, felt the wagon pitch forward from the trough of mud and grind freely on the beginning of this paving. He looked up with surprise and found they were passing under a great gate of logs into a stockade. The town rose ahead.

A tall, gangling fellow stood beside the gate leaning on the longest-barreled flintlock Robert had ever seen. He watched them go by with keen interest.

"Going in?" he called out. They gave him no answer, but he came shambling after them like a big loose-limbed hound. "Get the Indians?" he asked Robert. "Get burnt out?"

Calvin tied the two horses to a hitching post near the first cabin. "No," he said, turning to their welcomer to the town of Dorchester. "No Indians."

"You're lucky . . . you're lucky, I'd say, yes, sir," the boy drawled sagely. He had two flaxen "dog ears" of hair flopping one on each side of his face. His very pale skin was covered all over with freckles and what looked like gunpowder marks. He gave a high-pitched cackle: "Plenty of Indians about, plenty—all of 'em looking for hair." He laughed again. "Everybody's coming into town from up country. Thought you was too."

"What are the Indians doing, then?" Agatha asked him.

The boy studied her for the first time and snickered. "What'll them old savages ever do, Missis?" He lifted one of his "dog ears" with one hand and slashed at it with the edge of the other hand, making a grimace, too closely true to the face of a man being tortured. Then he dropped his hands and gave a whoop. "Aw, those Frenchies got the savages all properly stirred up. Look over yonder!"

He pointed where two objects dangling from poles slanted over the top of the stockade. At that distance they might have been flies strung from a spider's web or a pair of crows hung up to scare others off the corn. "Them's Indians," the boy said. "Dead uns. Don't go too close. They's whiffy!"

While he had been speaking a crowd had gathered around the cart. One of the men came forward, took Calvin's hand and shook it in a strangely formal manner without speaking. This was repeated by four or five of the other men. Two of the women also came forward, took Agatha by the arm and pressed it, greeting her once more without saying a word.

They were dressed, these citizens of Dorchester, in the poorest clothes, some in a mere patchwork of different rags; many wore leggings or blouses of animal hide. Most of the men were fully bearded, a sight Robert had seldom seen in England or in New York.

Still without a word, these strangers had now set about unloading the cart and unhitching the horses and the goats. They led the animals away without any protest from Calvin and then took charge of the party itself. It appeared to have been arranged beforehand who would take each of them. Robert was singled out by one of the women, a short lady with a brown, wizened face but kindly expression. She led him away with a firm grip on his arm, again giving no word of invitation, to a cabin on the far side of the stockade.

At the cabin door three boys and two girls lined themselves up. They shook hands with Robert in turn, just as formally as the men had greeted Calvin at the gate. Only the woman now broke the spell of silence: "We bid you greeting in God's name," she said.

After that she introduced her family one by one: Abel Butterfield, Joel and Paul, then the two girls, Rachel and Sarah Butterfield. The boys bowed, the girls dropped curt-

seys. Robert, too, bobbed back to each of them as they were
named, hoping he was showing the proper manners in this
strange figure of a country dance being performed at the back
door of a cabin in the middle of the American wilderness.

"What are we to call you, then?" his hostess asked kindly.

"Jack, Madame, if you please," Robert said after a second's
hesitation. "Jack Allen."

Once the formal ceremony was over, broad smiles had
replaced the solemn expressions on the faces of the Butterfield children. Two of the boys took Robert, one holding
each hand, and hurried him inside the cabin, while the
youngest, Paul, and the two girls danced about him, calling
out to their friends in nearby cabins.

Robert was taken to the back of the single room in which
the family lived. Here Abel and Joel brought him water in a
wooden tub. Robert took off his clothes, so ragged by this
time, it seemed that only the thorough basting of mud kept
the various scraps together. He pried off his broken boots and
unwound the strips of rag soaked in chicken fat he had put on
in order to keep off the frostbite. Then he washed himself
thoroughly. After the warm bath he stood bare by the roaring
fire, drying quickly, his whole body clean and tingling.

His clothes had been scooped up by the boys, who had run
off with them. In a few moments the three of them returned
holding up, as if in triumph, a pair of leather leggings, a blue
wool shirt, a pair of wool hose and two wooden clogs.

Warm, clean and comfortable, Robert sat down an hour
later to his first meal with the Butterfield family.

Robert liked Dorchester from the first day. Within a week
he had come to feel strangely at home in this raw frontier
town with its hard-working daily life, its few comforts and its
contrastingly formal manners. Though the work still lasted
from first light until sundown, it had ceased to be drudgery.
For one thing the Butterfields were quick to tell him how
much help his work was to them. Then, too, Robert found

that one quickly became known for any job one could do well. One morning a neighbor of the Butterfields came to the cabin to ask if he could borrow Jack Allen to help him make some repairs to the parchment and frame windows of his cabin. When Mr. Butterfield replied that the neighbor had better speak to Jack Allen himself, Robert felt, for the first time, like a free man.

Often, too, he would have company while he worked. If he split kindling near the house, Sarah and Rachel would sit at the cabin door to watch him and to chatter while they mended clothes or prepared food. When the boys went for wood to the forest they would go off together. Though they stayed at the edge, keeping the stockade in sight, the element of danger sharpened all their senses. It needed only the sound of a squirrel scampering up a tree trunk to bring them all on guard, imagining Indians everywhere among the fallen trees and brush.

Nearer the stockade, on several afternoons when they had finished their chores, Robert and Abel would practice shooting together. Robert found Mr. Butterfield's long-barreled musket awkward to handle. The first time he fired it, it must have leaped in his hands, and they could find no trace of the bullet near the white blaze on a tree which they used as a target. Powder and shot were scarce, but Abel generously allowed him another try, and he showed him once again how to keep the stock firm to his shoulder, how to aim and how to squeeze the trigger without pulling it. This time he hit the bottom of the blaze. Joel and Paul, who had come to watch, cheered. But Robert knew well enough that to hit a blaze on a tree not thirty feet away was one thing, but to hit an Indian moving quickly through cover to attack him, showing only a few inches of his body, and then for a second or two, was something else entirely.

After that he spent hours practicing on his own by the stockade until he could pour out the right amount of powder from the powder horn, prime, cap, load and sight, all in a matter of seconds. For his aiming he had to be content with throwing pebbles at a mark, but his eye grew surer and quicker.

In those early weeks at Dorchester he heard a good deal about the Indians from Abel, Joel, Mr. Butterfield and from some of those whose cabins had been threatened or attacked.

Much of what was most frightening about the Indian ways Robert learned from one of the refugees named Henry Bentall. He was a tall, thin, sick-looking man, with hair that was almost white, although he was only thirty. Before coming to America he had been a schoolmaster in Bath. When he heard that someone who had been in England only six months before had arrived at Dorchester he came and sought Robert out at the Butterfields.

They soon became friends. They would sit on boxes by the door of the schoolmaster's cabin mending a pile of harness for neighbors and talking—of England, or the Indians, or of the books they had read.

That Bath and Bower in Lancashire were at almost opposite ends of England did not seem to matter to Henry Bentall. He was anxious to learn everything Robert could tell him about the country he himself had left nearly seven years before. What surprised Robert as they talked of Bower, the Hall and all he had seen and done in the last months before the ambush in the gorge was that much of what he said made the schoolmaster sigh with homesickness for his own part of the country, while Robert found he had lost some, at any rate, of the yearning for the old life that had been so much in his thoughts, even in his dreams, in the hold of *The Charming Betty* and in the first weeks in America.

For his part, Robert was anxious to learn all he could from the schoolmaster about living in the wilderness. But though Henry Bentall was quite willing to talk about the Indians, he shied away quickly from any question about his own life since he had left England. In the end it was Calvin who succeeded where Robert had failed.

One spring evening Calvin had come looking for Robert and had found him talking to the schoolmaster. For a while he stood and listened to their conversation. Then he interrupted to question Henry Bentall about the farm he had left behind when he fled to the town. In the beginning the schoolmaster evaded all Calvin's questions with a wry smile. Once he said ironically, "I'll take my dying of fever or starvation in the towns, Mr. Moore, but I'll never lie awake half the night again in the middle of nowhere pondering which of the owl cries I hear are true owls and which are savages about to put steel to my throat."

Calvin shrugged his shoulders, not bothering to hide his contempt, and renewed his questioning, speaking more bluntly than before. In the end he found out what he wanted to know—that there was a well-built log hut with a dozen acres of cleared land, good soil for Indian corn, a heavy crop of squash, sweet potatoes and pumpkins, now abandoned in the wilderness.

"And you're welcome to it, Mr. Moore, if you choose to have it," the schoolmaster said, exasperated and out of patience. "You'll need no key; the door is open. I hope it brings you good fortune. I hope you become the richest man in America. . . ." He paused, catching sight of Calvin's expression, an idea of his own coming into his head at about the same time. "Will you take the boy with you?"

"Jack? He comes with me," Calvin said. Henry Bentall turned and grimaced at Robert. Robert had looked up, catching his breath at Calvin's words. Quite suddenly he realized he had ceased to be a free man talking to other free men; he was Calvin's bondservant and nothing more.

"When do you go, Mr. Moore?" Henry Bentall was asking.

"If it's hard enough in two days' time we'll be on our way," Calvin answered. "You say your cabin is no more than a few days' journey from Fort Charles. Why didn't you go *there?*"

"I had no liking for it," the schoolmaster said.

Calvin shrugged again. "You're a man of fancy tastes to my

mind," he said and he left them. They found little to talk about after he had gone.

The following evening Calvin goaded the schoolteacher into making out a deed, transferring his property to Calvin for the token sum of one dollar. The paper was signed and witnessed by six of the men of the town. As soon as the deed was his, Calvin showed a completely different mood. He became almost talkative, and because there was no one else he could talk to he sought out Robert.

"I've tested the ground and it's solid enough. Be ready tomorrow, eh?" Robert nodded, struggling to keep hidden the rebellion he felt. Calvin clapped the folded paper with one hand. "See this, boy—that's land!" he said triumphantly. As he stumped off into the darkness, Robert followed him with his glance, thinking how clumsy and ugly he looked, thinking, too, how unjust it was to be chained to such a bear of a man for a master.

Robert strolled twice around Dorchester before going back to the Butterfields' cabin to tell them he would be leaving in the morning.

Before dawn on the next day, Robert shook hands with Mr. Butterfield and thanked him. He bowed to Mrs. Butterfield and the girls, Sarah and Rachel. They were all very sleepy. Mrs. Butterfield said they were sure to see him again and he knew he would always be welcome to come and stay for as long as he wanted. Abel gave him his best hunting knife. Paul said he hoped he would meet some Indians and kill them; the others hushed him to be quiet. Very formally, one by one, they took his hand and wished him "God be with you." Robert went sadly off. He turned around twice to see his friends lined up by the door of the cabin.

While he was helping Calvin to load the cart, Henry Bentall came up to say goodbye. He gave Robert a book as a parting gift. "It's Defoe's *Robinson Crusoe*," he said. "You'll find it good wilderness reading. You may find the farm familiar too, if you know the book; I learned all the little farming and husbandry I had out of Defoe. Perhaps that was part of the trouble," he added wistfully, "too many books for this sort of country." Robert took the book and thanked him.

Henry Bentall was about to go, when he turned back. "Leave these two!" he whispered urgently. "Leave them as soon as you can and come back here. This stockade isn't much, I grant you, but it's something. The town may be safe . . . for it's certain to come!"

In the light of early morning, the schoolteacher's disheveled white hair and his sick face gave him the look of a madman and his words chilled Robert. "What will come?" Robert asked.

"The attack! One moment when you least expect it. They'll come while you sleep. . .. No, but be careful. Good luck. Get back here if you can. Goodbye . . ."

He took Robert's hand in his own cold hands, then he left quickly.

"'What did he say, that soft-skinned fool?" Calvin snarled. But he waited for no answer. "Come on!" Agatha and Calvin climbed onto the seat in front; Robert got in the back. They started up, drove along the main street where the first sunlight was coloring the lines of cabins, then under the long bar of the gate, the shadow of which slipped over the passing cart like a loop of rope. The long-haired boy who had welcomed them to Dorchester was sleeping soundly in the guard point, the sunlight glittering along the barrel of his gun.

It was well into May now and the weather was warm and dry. The surface of the trail had hardened and they made good progress. Robert soon noticed a change in the country. Between Calvin's farm and Dorchester most of their way had been through woodlands, but now the trail ran through a single forest. There were few clearings. It was often as dark at midday under the great pine trees or among groves of mixed oak, ash and birch trees as it might be an hour after sundown. And it was still. Even the occasional chatter of blue jays or the tapping of a woodpecker that started up for a few minutes and then stopped abruptly only seemed to emphasize this stillness.

At night, lying awake by the soft gray and glowing red of the pine-knot fire, Robert would listen for hours to the owls. Sometimes it seemed they had taken on the voices of people lost in the forest, calling out to one another for comfort and help, a little afraid of the sound of their own voices. Often the hooting would die away altogether and he would think they were gone. Then a flurry would start up in a tree above him, and a shape would sail slowly across the patch of sky bright with stars between the peaks of the pine trees.

On such nights as these the words of Henry Bentall about lying awake in his cabin, wondering which of the hooting calls he heard were of true owls and which were savages, would come back to Robert.

They were five days out of Dorchester on a morning that was as hot as a day in July. Agatha drove the cart. Calvin and Robert walked, one on either side, where the trail would let them. Calvin carried an axe over his shoulder to cut back any branches blocking the path. There had been no conversation for hours, but this was usual. The trail had been climbing since early that morning. The flies and mosquitoes were out in force. The horses were sweating freely and a swarm of insects had gathered around each of them. Agatha, sitting on the driving seat of the wagon, was several feet higher than the others.

The first indication Robert had that anything was wrong was when the cart stopped abruptly and he saw Agatha rising slowly to her feet, still holding the reins and staring ahead with a fixed expression of horror.

Calvin went to the back of the wagon, took his musket and loaded quickly and deliberately. He gave Robert the big skinning knife and they started forward. The woods had never seemed so still to Robert as they did at that moment. He wondered how his legs could move him so easily forward while everything else seemed to hold him back.

They had only a little way to go. A man lay dead, stretched out as he had fallen. The two bullet holes looked very small in the middle of his back, but the top of his head was one red and open wound. His pockets had been turned out and there were scraps of paper lying about in the grass. His boots had been taken. His horse lay dead a few yards on. "Ambushed!" Calvin said curtly. "From over there."

Robert lifted his eyes to follow the direction of Calvin's arm, half expecting to meet the eyes of the man's murderers. All the woods were theirs now; every patch of forest might conceal them. Calvin knelt down and touched the body. "Not long ago," he said. "Probably this morning."

They climbed up the slope beside the track and found a shelf of rock. Here, thought Robert, the Indians had lain in wait, hidden in this dark patch under two hemlocks until the man came riding along down there only ten yards away in bright sunlight. The down of a feather lay on the rock. Calvin stooped, picked it up and pulled it apart with his thumbnail.

At that moment something made a sudden rush close by. Calvin spun about, bringing the gun up to his shoulder and firing. There was an explosion, shattering the silence, then the thud of a bullet striking home and the sound of a heavy fall.

Everything had been too quick for Robert to react. Now nothing further happened. Smoke drifted away through the trees. Calvin cursed: "It was nothing, nothing, I think, but a deer," he said. "But that was a fine sound to rally the savages!"

He loaded once more and then they walked forward to a clump of hazel bushes. Sure enough, in the middle lay a young buck, shot cleanly and quite dead; he had only just begun to show his horns. Robert lifted the body and found it heavy.

The wagon stood in the lane and the horses were waiting when they returned, but there was no sign of Agatha. Calvin called her name, not loudly. Then they saw her come up out of the bushes, walk to the wagon and lean limply against the wheel. "Why did you fire? Why did you fire?" she asked.

Her bonnet had tilted to one side, her face was colorless and shone with perspiration, her hair hung lank and disordered. Robert had never seen anyone look as ill as Agatha did at that moment. He would have said something to her, but he could think of nothing to say. Calvin made no attempt to comfort her.

Robert took the buck and put it in the back of the wagon. Then he and Calvin lifted up the dead man and carried him by stages to the wagon, where they laid him down on the soft belly of the buck. They covered the back of the man's head with a piece of sacking.

"Come on!" Calvin said. "Let's be off. If the savages heard the shot, they heard it. The fort can't be far." He flicked up the horses to relieve his own feelings and they were off again, Calvin and Agatha sitting together on the cart, Robert walking beside it holding the gun.

It was probably no farther than another mile when they came suddenly and unexpectedly out of the narrow trail and onto a broad log and dirt road. "This is the highway," Calvin said, "the new military road I heard of in New York. We'll soon be at the fort. Nothing will happen here."

They turned into the road as he spoke. It was strange to see the walls of the forest open out after so long, but it was the same forest; they were not out of it, despite Calvin's words, and Robert felt just as much on his guard.

They had traveled for only two hours in this new way, however, when they came to a stockade with a closed gate. Above this, high on a pole against a sky clear of all trees, waved the red, white and blue colors of the Union Jack.

9

The Empty House
in the Wilderness

ROBERT WAS TO KNOW Fort Charles well in the year that
followed, but he never saw any reason to change his first bad
impression of the place. The setting itself was fine enough.
The fort stood on a bluff at the bend of a river, so that it was
protected by water on two sides. Beyond the river on the far
side there was a wide brown belt of marshland and reed
before the forest began again. Then, far away in the distance
above the miles of black trees rose a range of mountains with
white peaks.

Nearer at hand, however, the first thing Robert was conscious of was the smell of the skins that were drying on
frames. He noticed a general air of disorder as well: broken
wagons, piles of timber and refuse of all sorts were packed
between the cabins and even under the guard posts of the
stockade. Chickens and pigs ran about freely underfoot, and
faded rags of clothing hung from every hook and window.

They had been questioned closely for some minutes before
the man on guard would open the gate to them. Inside, they
found no welcoming committee. Instead, a crowd of five
men, armed with guns and knives, watched them from a
distance. One of them, a huge man with a spade beard, came
to the back of the wagon, turned over the body of the dead
man and called out with little show of concern, "They got

Rowley." He looked at Calvin and grinned unpleasantly. "That's the third messenger of ours they've scalped. You were lucky. Where'd you find him, Mister What-ever-your-name is?"

No one helped them here to unload the wagon. The crowd stood looking on with dull or contemptuous stares, as though the arrival provided them with some slight interest and amusement in lives that had little of either.

"Leave most of it on," Calvin said. Since no one had offered them room for the night, it seemed likely they would sleep as usual under the wagon, right there in the middle of the square.

"Here's a fine Christian place!" Robert heard Calvin mutter under his breath. "We'll build a fire here," he said, "and cook the buck. Then we'll see what they say. Get us some water, Jack."

Robert took the bucket and set off across the square. He could see where the well stood up near the drying frames on the other side of the fort, and he was glad he had no need to ask where it was. As he walked the smell grew stronger and whole swarms of flies came up to meet him.

But something else had caught his attention.

He had thought from a distance that there were hides drying on all the frames. Now he saw that on one of the frames it was not an animal skin that was stretched out but the body of a human being. Unconscious of the hostile looks he had drawn and feeling sick with disgust and foreboding, Robert turned slightly and walked up to this particular frame.

Closer still, he discovered it was a boy of about his own age and size. He was tied to the frame by the wrists and ankles, naked except for a string of blue beads around his neck and a breechcloth of colored leather; his body was covered with red weals, but he was alive.

A pair of sharp black eyes were pretending to look through

Robert. The boy's mouth tightened, however, as though he were bracing himself for a blow.

Robert stood watching him for a minute, struggling with his own feelings. Then he walked on to the well, filled the bucket at the pump, came back, and used a scoop to bring the water carefully to the boy's dry lips. The Indian swallowed quickly, now looking into Robert's eyes, though neither of them said a word. Then Robert noticed the other boy flicker his eyes as a signal and then dart his glance over Robert's shoulder. Robert turned.

As he did so a hand screwed up his collar and spun him about again. He felt himself lifted clear, then kicked hard, and he went sprawling head down in the dust. Before he recovered, he was doused with water. The big man with the spade beard stood over him and pushed him down again each time he tried to get to his feet. "Go to your wagon, you bond-brat! If you like savages so well, we'll build you a frame to stretch on yourself." He kicked Robert again and walked off. There was a stale laugh or two from the loafers as Robert scrambled to his feet.

He picked up the bucket, filled it at the pump and returned to the wagon. He was shaking as he walked and his face burned. He struggled to control his anger, telling himself to wait; he could do nothing for the moment. But his anger would not cool. Fortunately Calvin accepted the state he was in without questioning.

They skinned the buck, divided it and cooked the best of it on a spit over an open fire as Calvin had said they would do right there in the square. The smell attracted a good crowd, but the loafers stood a little way off and watched—like a circle of dogs, Robert thought. The same idea must have been in Calvin's mind as he put an obvious relish into his eating. But Robert was in no mood to enjoy the food. Whenever he looked up he could see the top of the frame across the square, where the Indian boy was stretched out in the sun with the smell and the flies. He cut off a large piece of meat and wrapped it up to put inside his shirt.

Evening came and Robert returned to the pump for more water. This time there was no chance of approaching near enough to the frame to give the boy the meat. Two of the witnesses of his early beating were still on the watch. One of them taunted him while he pumped the water into the bucket. "No good feeding that buck," he said, sneering. "He's to be stretched out for good tomorrow."

Robert went on pumping as though he had heard nothing. "Caught day before yesterday, pretended he'd come in to trade, spying out the guard posts," the man went on. Robert hurried to be away, but the loafer came and caught him by the sleeve. This time his voice changed to a nasal whine. "He's the cub of those French savages, like the ones that killed old Rowley. You brought him in. Tell me, boy, was *he* so pretty?" The loafer was almost pleading now: "What you want to go and give those murderers drink for?"

Robert bit his lip but said nothing in reply. He stepped around his questioner and walked on. But he did not go directly back to the wagon. Instead, he went to the parapet at the rear of the fort. Here there was only a single line of sharpened stakes about six feet high. Robert climbed up and stood looking out across the river. Waterfowl were calling to one another in the reeds with harsh voices. A great V of wild geese flew overhead, but it was so dark by now that he could hear them better than he could see them. The line of mountains was still visible, with the band of black forest under the pale peaks. Robert stood there for almost a quarter of an hour, until it was quite dark, until the sky was covered with stars, the waterfowl had fallen silent and the night cold had started to come up from the river. All these minutes by himself had given him a chance to think.

It was somewhere near the middle of the night when Robert moved inch by inch out of his blankets, listening all the time to the breathing of his two companions. Freeing himself, he crawled quickly by the shortest route from the wagon to the stockade. He was now under the guardwalk, immediately beneath the feet of the sentries and out of their sight for most of the distance to his goal. He moved fast, barefoot, keeping close to the long wall, gripping the knife Abel Butterfield had given him so tightly his knuckles began to ache.

He came to the first of the cabins. Here he had to double himself up to pass below the line of the windows. As he did so he heard breathing scarcely a foot away across the sill; it sounded like a woman's. As he held his own breath and tiptoed past, the thought came to him that if he had been an Indian, he could have stood where he was, put his arm over the sill and plunged the knife into the woman on the other side.

A feeling of guilt and confusion came over him. He wondered whether what he was doing was right. Then he remembered how he had been trussed up himself in the wagon after the ambush and again when he had tried to escape from Calvin. He thought too of the gibbets at Dorchester. Far from certain of himself, he decided to go on.

He was beyond the cabin now. A man standing on the guardwalk might have looked inside the fort and seen him. All the same he would have to take the risk. At worst it was no more than thirty yards in the open to the first frame.

He made the distance as quickly as possible. When he was among the frames he could walk upright without the likelihood of being seen. Even in the cold night air the rancid smell of the hides was strong.

The Indian boy had heard him coming. His flesh was so cold when Robert brushed against it he wondered whether the Indian would be too weakened by exposure even to walk. Robert felt for the boy's bonds and cut carefully through them. As he was released the Indian fell forward.

"Aiee," he said softly to himself. He took the sides of the

frame and pulled himself up on them. Then he moved his arms about, lifted his knees one after the other and rubbed his joints with his fingers. Once he ducked his head down quickly between his knees as though he felt himself about to faint. All the time he was moving, the Indian grunted away softly to himself.

After a short while he gave Robert a nod as if to say he was now ready. Robert took his hand and led him to the point at the rear of the fort where he had stood looking out over the river earlier in the evening. The Indian's hand felt numb with cold in Robert's. He was breathing as though the few steps had cost him a great effort.

Robert was sure they had failed.

Just then an arm was thrown around his shoulder and the other boy gave him a playful squeeze. "Can you get home?" Robert whispered anxiously. There was no answer in English, only another playful squeeze, followed by a few words he did not understand. However, the Indian boy looked up at the line of stakes and signaled, with an unmistakable sweep of his eyes, that he wanted to get up and over.

To help him, Robert got down so the Indian could use him as a step. With care, the Indian placed his foot in the middle of Robert's back, then vaulted over. Robert heard him drop on the far side, but he made surprisingly little sound doing so.

Robert stood looking over the spikes, expecting to find the Indian boy had gone. Instead he stood waiting for him on the other side. For a second Robert was half tempted to follow— to go with him, or to find his own way back to England. When the Indian boy realized he was not coming, he came closer to the wall. "Goodbye," he said; then he said something in his own language, adding finally, *"Merci, Monsieur, merci."* With this he turned and set off through the long grass for the bluff and the river. He made very little noise and in a minute he was gone. The night seemed suddenly empty to Robert.

The minute Robert was inside his blankets again, he fell asleep. He had a strange dream. For the first time in months, he was back at the Hall, sitting in a great Jacobean chair at the head of the table. The table was covered with a banquet, which included the whole of the buck roasted on a great silver charger. On one side of him sat the Newt and on the other the Indian boy. Then he saw his father rise up at the far end of the table, lifting his glass. "Be upstanding," his father called out, "and drink to the heir of the Entricks! To my son—to Robert Entrick!" Then the Newt got up and the Indian boy stood; but right down both sides of the table Robert could see people sitting. He recognized Captain Mask and Calvin and his uncle, and he saw each of them was struggling to get up, but they were caught up in something and not one of them could stand.

He thought he was still dreaming when he felt himself being dragged roughly along by his feet.

It was early morning. He was standing in the square at Fort Charles, surrounded by a ring of figures. The big man with the spade beard who had kicked him the afternoon before was holding him close to his side now, talking to him.

"What we want to know," the man was asking, "is who let that savage of ours loose in the night. Did you?"

Robert, bleary still with sleep, looked at him without trying to answer. "*Did you?*" the man roared at him once more.

"Yes," Robert said, "I did."

"By heaven," someone else whistled. The man who gripped Robert now flung him violently to the ground.

"What's this?" Calvin asked, appearing beside them.

"Yes, *you!*" the leader said, turning to him. "Your brat let the savage loose, the Indian cub that was to be hung. Do you know why?"

Calvin looked around the ring of hostile faces, then considered Robert on the ground. He made no answer.

The leader again broke the silence: "All right, all right, we were set to string up the savage, now we'll string up this brat as a lover of savages and murderers. Get a rope!"

"No!" Calvin shouted. He barged his way through the circle and seized hold of Robert by the arms. "Come on," he said. "We're going."

Jacob scrutinized them both. "Get a pair of ropes!"

Calvin had never lacked courage. Everything stood at that moment perfectly balanced between him and Jacob. No one went for the rope and no one moved away from the circle which menaced Calvin and Robert. "Come on, you idiot!" Calvin said fiercely. He clubbed Robert with his open hand and sent him sprawling at the feet of the onlookers. Then he caught the boy up, slung him over his shoulder, carried him to the cart and flung him roughly in the back. He loaded the wagon, ordered Agatha on, swung himself up and started the horses—all in a few seconds but without appearing to rush himself; never looking, either, at the knot of men who stood undecided what to do.

"Gi-yap!" Calvin shouted to the horses. The cart went off for thirty yards and stopped by the gate. Then, miraculously, the gate opened. Robert lay still on the sacks at the bottom of the wagon. He heard shouting behind, then a dull thump, another, and a third. Something struck Calvin full in the back. He cursed and flicked the whip. The horses broke into a fast trot and the wagon lurched wildly about. Clods of dirt were raining all about them now. One of them crashed on the side of the cart, and there was a scatter of dirt and pebbles everywhere.

"Christians! God-fearing Christians, the lot of you!" Calvin shouted at the top of his voice, turning. "May the savages burn you here and in Hell hereafter!"

They jolted along for another mile or so and then stopped.

The horses were lathered, and the two surviving goats, who were tethered behind, had run themselves almost to death.

Robert expected Calvin's wrath to fall heavily upon him, now that the danger was over, but a curious change had come over his master. "Ha!" Calvin snorted, the nearest thing to a laugh Robert had ever heard him make. "Savages indeed! Who are they to call people savages, those wolves?" He picked up one of the goats and lifted it into the wagon, where it lay exhausted, looking up. "Hang us, would they?" Calvin went on. "Turn us off with all the laws and etiquette of Old England—ha!" He looked at Robert. "Did you let that savage boy go?"

"Yes, Mr. Moore, I did," Robert answered coolly.

"Then you're a fool! A born fool! I'll get no seven years' service from a dolt who's as set as you upon being hanged!"

Yet to his surprise and confusion, Robert found he had come close at long last to pleasing this strange man. There was no doubt about it, Calvin was flushed with excitement and pleasure.

To Robert's even greater surprise, when they started slowly off, Calvin began to sing. He sang "The Miller of Dee" in a deep, rolling, not unpleasant bass. Agatha, having recovered herself from her fright at the fort and her present astonishment, interrupted her husband to tell him the song was not seemly. Calvin paid no attention whatsoever.

"Can you sing, boy?" Calvin called out to Robert.

"Yes, Mr. Moore," Robert said, "and I know the verses of that song well enough."

"Then sing it!" Calvin bellowed.

And so, feeling at first like a fool, soon after as free of sensible everyday feelings as though he had drunk far too much cider, Robert opened his mouth wide and sang.

They went on through the forest as if Calvin were himself the Miller of Dee with his cart, his wife and his apprentice, as though they were rambling along with a load of flour, singing to pass the time of day, down some safe Cheshire lane far from Indians, near-hangings and all the waiting terrors of the wilderness.

Calvin followed the directions he had written down at Henry Bentall's dictation on the back of the deed. It was just as well that these were clear and that Calvin had a good eye for country, because the trail had now narrowed until it would only just take the width of the wagon, while its surface was very little worn. Several other lanes branched out through the trees, looking just as likely as the one they were on. Yet Calvin kept the direction he wanted and an occasional blaze mark on a tree showed he was right.

At about four one afternoon, some time before they had expected to arrive, they caught sight of the roof of a cabin standing at the far side of a clearing. Calvin stopped the horses. He and Robert went forward on foot.

They crossed a space of several acres which had once been cleared. Weeds and wild flowers of many colors brushed their knees. White butterflies fluttered about the meadow. Beyond the gentle slope on which the cabin stood there was a gleam of water.

Calvin was walking fast, taking a keen interest in everything he saw. They came up to the cabin. It was very small (it could not have contained more than one room), but there were bright green shutters across the two windows, something which made it look like a toy house—quite incongruous in the rough, forest landscape and almost pretty. Close to the doorway a dogwood tree was in full flower.

They tried the door and it swung gently open. Inside there was a musty smell like the inside of an old cupboard. Walking in, they broke through a screen of cobweb. By the light through the door Robert could see a box bed, a plank table, two benches and a cupboard. There was nothing else in the small room except for some clothes hanging from a hook on the far wall. These Calvin gathered up over his arm and took outside. They were women's dresses, faded now, ragged and damp, but the stuff was still firm and the lace that hung from one blue dress must once have been fine.

"Women's clothes? Can this be the cabin, Mr. Moore?" Robert asked.

"It can be! It is," Calvin said angrily.

"But the schoolmaster . . ." Robert began.

"You're a fool!" Calvin shouted, his face purple with rage. "This *is* the place. It's mine! I've the deed." Then, changing the tone of his voice, he went on: "It's the right position and it's empty enough. Look, boy, there's the creek your fool of a friend spoke of. And here are his acres cleared. Of *course* it's the place!"

Robert left him and walked around the cabin. In the back he came to a mound with a square of stones set before it like a terrace a few inches higher than the surrounding ground. There was a flat slab of wood on the front of the mound. Robert took this away and peered in. Inside the mound was hollow and lined with stones, dark and cool like a cellar. He put the door back in place. A double line of stakes ran back to the rear wall of the cabin, making what had once been a chicken run.

"It *is* the right place," he said to Calvin when he came back.

"Of course it is!" Calvin growled. "Here are the hills for Indian corn and the patches of squash." He screwed up his eyes in suspicion. "What makes you so sure that it's Bentall's cabin now?"

"He said it would be laid out like something in a book he gave me," Robert replied.

"Ha! Like a book is it!" Calvin humphed with contempt. "It would be. Well, he was no sort of farmer, that fool, but he built a good house; it's kept the winter out and the rats.

"There's work to be done here," Calvin said and he ground one hand against the other. "Work. Oh yes! But the soil's good, very good, some of it's river soil, the best a man could want. Come, let's see the place over!"

They walked together across the sloping field toward the creek. There was one mound in the middle of it, which stood up three feet above the surrounding ground. From the top of this they would have a good view of the cabin, the creek and the country around. As they made for this point they saw a slab of stone sticking up from the top of the hummock. Calvin took one look, then ignored the stone. Robert, however, had noticed that there were letters carved on the side of the rock and he bent down to read them. The words had been rough-carved and the light was falling full on them, casting no shadow; in places he had to feel out the inscription:

> Jennie Maria Bentall, née McAllison
> Sleep in this Wilderness. In God's Love Now—
> But O, Beyond Mine, 1755

"What is it you've found, Jack?" asked Calvin.

"This is his wife's grave," Robert answered quietly.

"The schoolmaster's? Then that explains the dresses." Calvin shielded his eyes against the glare of the sunlight and looked down at the stone.

"There's many stones like that one in the wilderness," he said, thinking aloud to himself. "And many men's wives left behind like that." Then he turned to Robert: "We'll make a beginning today, in the house at least. This stone and mound we'll leave. It's in the middle of the best land, but I'll move no graves," Calvin Moore said.

❧ 10 ❧

The Attack

As CALVIN HAD PROPHESIED, there was work to be done.

In the last days of May they cleaned out the cabin and set about clearing the rank growth of weeds off the land.

June started with a week of thunderstorms. Working even in heavy rain, they built up the corn hills and planted the seed corn Calvin had bartered for at Dorchester. With the rain came the mosquitoes. The insects followed them in clouds about the field, biting them until their faces and arms swelled and it was difficult to sleep at night.

After a week the weather settled into long, hot, unclouded days. Most of the mosquitoes went, their high-pitched wailing replaced by the unending sound of crickets and by the full chorus of birds. Robert had never heard such birdsong. Their colors too were brilliant. The clump of dogwood by the cabin was alive all day long with flashes of scarlet, orange and black, blue and white.

Robert took off his shirt to work, though Agatha said more than once that it was unholy and a manner fit only for savages. In fact, within a few weeks the sun had burned his body so brown that there was little to choose between him and the Indian boy he had freed at Fort Charles. He was taller now and he grew strong with the heavy work of hoeing, felling trees and dragging out stumps by the roots to clear new land.

July came, then August. The corn had sprung up from the late-planted seed, soft green or silky, pink stalks and leaves, already more than three feet high and growing so fast the change could be seen from one summer's day to the next.

The farm had been transformed by this time from the place they had found abandoned that May afternoon. Newly cleared land stretched for a hundred yards beyond the school-master's original cultivation. On one side this was fenced off from the forest wall. On the other, where the trees were smaller, more ground had been marked out for clearing during the winter.

In what time he had of his own, Robert had built himself a room against a wall of the cabin. At the moment it was open in front to a view of the falling ground and the creek, but the shelter would need another wall before winter. Meanwhile, there was no barrier between his life and the other life of the meadow and the forest. Chipmunks, squirrels, meadow mice and deer mice scampered across the dirt floor beneath the hammock where he slept. At night a screech owl made a kill, swooping through the room. From his hammock he saw the flocks of ducks and wild geese following the line of the stream. He went to sleep with the rasping of the crickets and woke to the chatter of birds.

September came. The corn ripened, red pumpkins grew fat, the squash flowered yellow, the first tree by the creek began to turn.

There was no lack of food in this rich country. They were too short of powder and shot to use it for hunting, but they caught fat trout in the creek and took pheasants, grouse, woodcock and wild turkeys in the snares they set.

In all this time there were no signs of the Indians. They had come close to forgetting about them with the work from first light to dusk and the way in which the farm was flowering up under their hands. Often Robert would see Calvin standing on top of the mound by the creek, looking over the land and what they had done. Though he stood on ground three feet above the surrounding field, the corn now

rose above his waist. "Jack, lad!" he called out across the
cornfield one day as he saw Robert coming. "What did your
schoolmaster say? He wished me the richest man in America!
Just look at the fat of this land!"

Only on Sunday was there something of a break from this
endless work. In the morning they accomplished what was
"needful and merciful," all that was allowed on the Sabbath.
In the afternoon Agatha would practice Robert in the cate-
chism from the *New England Primer,* the only book, except
for the Bible and *Poor Richard's Almanack,* which she considered it holy to read. In the later afternoon or early evening, as before, Calvin would read from the Bible.

As he listened to his flat, expressionless voice above the
cricket chorus one Sunday late in September, Robert's attention drifted for a while. He looked at Calvin and Agatha and
thought how changed they both were now from what they
had been on the day, four months before, when they had
arrived at the deserted cabin in the wilderness. Calvin had
become as brown as Robert from working in the sun. Even
Agatha, who kept herself carefully covered and hid her face
under a large bonnet that had once belonged to the schoolmaster's wife, looked a different person from the pale, fright-
ened woman she had been in the spring.

Robert brought his attention back to the words of the
Bible. Calvin had been reading of Jacob and his seven years'
labor for Rachel. At that moment, as he read, the farmer
seemed to Robert very much as one of the Old Testament
patriarchs must have been. Robert remembered, too, that his
own service was for seven years. How long had he worked for
Calvin? For barely seven months! And he was working for
the love of no Rachel—for nothing.

Then Calvin read on how Leman had tricked Jacob and
how he had given him his eldest daughter, Leah, for a wife
instead of Rachel, and how Jacob had had to begin again—
fourteen years!

Calvin finished and closed the book. He turned to Robert

and asked him to come out with him to the fields. Agatha raised her eyes and stared suspiciously from one of them to the other as Robert followed Calvin outside.

They walked together to the mound by the creek. It was just after sundown. The light was streaming back along the rows of corn, giving the leaves a glimmer of red gold. On the far side of the creek the pine trees looked as though they too were reflecting the full glow of a fire. The stream curled around the land beyond the hummock. A sumac tree was already a blood red against the blue water.

They had not spoken since leaving the cabin. Calvin appeared ill at ease, as though he had not sufficiently thought out what it was he wanted to say. Robert broke the silence to tell him the corn was almost ripe and that he was thinking of making a crib to hold the ears. Calvin listened but only nodded his head.

"It's a good farm," Calvin said at last. "It's the best land I've ever seen. I've worked for it and I've inherited it. That's justice. That's righteousness. That's the good bargain, the Covenant. I doubted once, but I doubt no more!"

The man stopped. He had been almost shouting his words across the cornfield, as though they were not meant for Robert but for someone else. His voice changed now. "What I mean to say, Jack," he said, turning, "is this: that when I die it must come to you. I have no son."

Caught by surprise, Robert said nothing. But Calvin seemed to expect no answer. "You must work for it. I worked for it. God is my witness to that. I worked! But if you work, you shall have it all in time. I'll make out the deed." He stopped, uncertain how to go on. "That is what I meant to say to you, Jack."

"Thank you, Mr. Moore," Robert managed. But Calvin's mood had changed; his brow came down again in a black frown.

"It's no gift to you, so save your gentleman's manners!

Come back to the house now. And tomorrow do what you said—begin a crib for the corn. We'll harvest this week."

All the following day Robert worked building the crib. He split a great log with a hammer and a set of iron wedges. When he had planks he split these again until they were no more than six inches wide. With the rails he built up a frame against the far wall of his own room. In time he would build a double wall around the crib and stuff the crack between with tightly packed corn silk. For the moment he simply constructed shelves of cross-slats so the ears would be well above the ground, spread out on the shelves. Raised up on stilts, the corn would be out of the way of mice, chipmunks and squirrels, and to make sure they would not use the uprights to climb up, he put a wide circle of wood as a shield on each one. It took him hours of work to make the set of the roof as he wanted it, slanted so the rain and the weight of the snow would shift off it, letting some air in, but tight enough to keep out the birds and the animals. By the time the crib was finished it was after sundown, but Agatha, furious he was so late coming in, sent him to bed without a meal. He was up before dawn the next day to start work on the walls.

On the first of October, by Agatha's calculations from the marks she made in her almanac, they started to harvest the corn. Calvin and Robert began at first light at the creek and worked up the rows toward the cabin. They spread out blankets and filled them with the ears as they stripped the stalks. Agatha followed them, cutting off the stalks and carrying the waste to a point near the creek where the fire was burning. They worked all day in this manner, with only a short break at noon to lunch on goat's-milk cheese and fruit.

The hours wore on. They carried the full blankets many times to the crib. On one expedition Calvin made a careful examination of the crib. "That's good," he said—the first compliment he had ever paid to Robert's work.

The sun burned, their backs ached, the loud chirping of

the crickets fretted them, but the rows never seemed to come to an end. Late in the afternoon, Agatha returned to the cabin. An hour or so later, Calvin also dropped out, calling to Robert as he did so to come in soon for the evening meal or he would miss it once more. But Robert hardly heard his words. He was working on doggedly, playing at a game of his own. He wanted to fill the whole of his crib with corn that first night, and there was only one shelf left to fill.

The light was beginning to fail. When he looked up once he could see the fireflies glowing in the ferns by the side of the woods. He was far from the creek now, working twenty yards from the fence between the rows of the tallest corn. As he worked, he became gradually aware of another sound above the crickets, the low bubbling sound of wild turkeys. They must be quite nearby, he thought to himself; perhaps a flock of them had come to feast off the stray ears of corn that lay scattered on the ground between the rows. He would remember to get some snares set for them tomorrow.

Gobble, gobble, gobble—they were getting very close now, he thought a minute or two later; perhaps he could catch one that night. Then he froze.

Crawling along the ground between the rows of corn was a man, not ten yards away—a man bare to the waist, with two feathers set in his hair, a gun in his hand. The man moved forward like a snake, but as he coiled and uncoiled over the ground he made the sound Robert had been hearing for the last ten minutes, the gobbling of a wild turkey.

From other rows all around the spot where Robert stood the same noise came, but he could see only the one warrior now moving away down the row. It had grown much darker. Beyond the cornfield there was the glimmer of the stream, and against it showed the outline of the roof of the cabin. Robert held his breath and listened to the sound of the gobbling. All of it now came from between him and the cabin. Perhaps the Indians had passed him. It seemed impossible that they had missed him. He tried to think how much noise he had been making. Maybe they had left a guard behind who was watching him at that very moment, ready to strike him down the instant he moved or gave the alarm. He tried to look about without moving so much as a leaf of the corn.

All at once the thought of Agatha and Calvin sitting inside, knowing nothing of what was coming, was too much for Robert.

"Indians!" he screamed. "Indians!" He leaped through the screen of corn into the next row, ducked against any blow, crashed through another row of corn, weaved and tacked in and out of the plants like an animal, stopping and shouting from time to time at the top of his voice.

But by now other sounds had come to his ears—wild yells, shots: the attack had begun. Robert turned and raced straight for the cover of the forest.

He reached the split-rail fence. A short hoe was leaning up against one of the posts. He grabbed this, vaulted over the rail and plunged into the wall of ferns. Once in cover, he ran in a wide arc and came back through the woods to a point where he could see the back of the cabin, hoping he might be able to give help to the others even then.

But as the outline of the house appeared, a tongue of flame shot up from it, sending a shower of sparks across the sky. The savages were whooping now; one of them let out a cry, clapping his tongue to make a wild belling. There were shots, shrieks, then one long, frantic scream, finally the crash of timbers falling.

Robert turned and ran wildly into the woods. He crashed through branches, collided with trunks of trees, tripped more than once and fell violently on his face. Each time he scrambled up immediately and ran on, putting what distance he could between himself and the fire, the yelling Indians and the screams.

He sprinted until he ran himself out. Even here he could smell burning. When he turned his head there was the red

glow between the trees. Not far enough, he decided. If any
Indians had followed him, the noise he had made would have
given him away, even if it was too dark now to see him. He
took a deep breath and got up. This time he moved far more
deliberately, no longer in a rush of fear. Even so twigs cracked
under his feet; branches struck him with a loud thump, and
the sounds seemed to carry a long way. All the while he was
clutching the short hoe in his hand like a weapon, searching
out every shape and shadow for an enemy.

Robert had gone no more than a hundred yards in this way
when the woods began to thin out. He was walking now on a
thick carpet of moss that muffled the sound of his footsteps.
By slowing down a little he found he could move so that he
made no noise at all. Ahead, through a clump of bushes, he
saw water gleaming: he had come back to the creek.

He chose a big spruce whose roots knotted over the bank.
Using the roots for cover, he crawled to the water and looked
upstream and down. A full harvest moon was shining, light-
ing the creek. Twenty yards downstream there was a small
shingle beach. Drawn up, halfway out of the water, were four
war canoes. Robert might never have seen the guard if the
two long strands he had taken for the leaves of a plant on the
bank had not dipped at that moment against the water so
that he noticed the profile of the man below them.

For some reason the close presence of the Indian now gave
him no feeling of fear. Without hesitating, and making no
sound, he eased his way through the cage of roots and
lowered himself inch by inch into the water. The creek came
to his waist. The water was icy cold and flowing fast, but the
bottom was firm under his feet. He waited, looked about and
listened, trying to discover if there were any other guards.
Then he slipped down into the water. Keeping his eyes above
the surface, he half swam, half walked to the nearest canoe.
Under the cover of the boat he moved up the beach, until he
crouched no more than the width of the boat away from the

guard. Once again, he drew in a deep breath, stood up, raised
the hoe in both hands above him and crashed it down as hard
as he could on the skull of the Indian.

Without waiting to see if the guard was dead, he flung the
hoe into the boat, gripped both sides with his hands, drove it
off the shingle with all his strength and jumped in. The
canoe swept forward, rocking dangerously, caught the current,
steadied itself and swung off into the center of the stream.

Robert found a paddle and worked his way carefully to the
stern. The stream was brilliantly lit by the moon. He could
see the trees on both banks as they slipped by. The canoe was
moving fast and straight. Within a matter of minutes the
current would carry him past the cabin. He wondered
whether to try to turn the boat about and paddle upstream,
but the flow was too strong; he would have to go on.

He passed the big red sumac tree. Then he came to the
smoldering piles of cornstalks Agatha had been burning.
Now the trees on the left bank stopped. The cabin came into
view, still fiercely alight. All the ground around the building
showed clearly in the glow and the moonlight, but there was
not an Indian to be seen. Robert had slipped down into the
bottom of the canoe, where he lay peering cautiously over the
side. Now he lifted himself up a little. The boat had come
abreast of the mound in the cornfield, and this cut off his
view of the cabin. It would probably serve just as well to hide
him.

But all the time he had been looking at the level of the
bank. At that moment something caused him to raise his eyes.
There on the top of the mound by the grave of the schoolmaster's wife stood three figures. All three of the Indians
were looking out into the stream. They must have seen him
by now! The moonlight was so bright he could make out
their features quite clearly. All these seconds he was passing
in front of them, very slowly it seemed, suspended, quite
helpless, perhaps twenty yards in front of them, and all the

while they continued to stare straight at him, still making no move.

Something dark came down, cutting them off; the trees had started again on the bank. He could see the Indians no longer, and the spell of the last seconds had been broken.

11

The Endless Wilderness

THE MOMENT he recovered himself, Robert began to paddle.
He had no idea where he was going. It was enough to be
moving so quickly away from what had happened in the last
half hour.

He turned around once and saw the glow of the fire, a red
arc, breathing like the mouth of a furnace among the dark
trees. Back there the house was still burning, the corn bin
filled with corn, his shelter—everything. Calvin and Agatha
were dead; probably that was the best he could hope for
them. Everything the schoolmaster had prophesied had come
true. The land had fattened only to waste in fire.

He paddled on until his body grew warmer under the wet
clothes. He knew that Fort Charles stood beside a stream (at
that moment he was thinking only of the protecting stockade,
not of Jacob and the men who had done their best to hang
him). But was the fort above the cabin or below it? Was it
even on the same stream? Without Calvin's map he was lost.
He remembered, however, that streams flowed ultimately in
the direction of the sea. At least, he comforted himself, he
was going toward the English settlements and not deeper and
deeper into the wilderness of the Indians.

He had mastered the handling of the delicately balanced
craft. Swinging the paddle from one side to the other with
quick, smooth movements, overarm, underarm, he took a
chunk of black water each time with the blade, pulling the
boat on. His body felt warm, but there was a cool breeze on

his face. The dark screen of trees seemed to break apart to let him pass.

After half an hour's paddling, all his feelings seemed to have changed. It was as though he had forgotten the farm, forgotten the horror of the attack, the death of the two people he had lived with for so long. He felt only a great wave of elation passing over him, a feeling of pure adventure.

This time he was alone. Whatever the circumstances were that had brought it about, he had escaped, he was free, he was on his own. He had struck off absolutely alone into the heart of the wilderness! And with what? With the wet rags he wore, a short hoe, the stolen canoe . . . He was more shipwrecked than Robinson Crusoe, here in the middle of America, with its woods full of murderous savages, a wilderness that appeared to have no paths and no limits. Without a compass! Without a chart! Without a gun! Robert Entrick, who had once been afraid of riding alone at night three miles between school and home, who had thought the whole world had come to an end when he was kidnapped, who had hesitated to run away when he had been given the chance outside the inn in Liverpool because he felt unsure of himself in a strange town!

He began to feel as he had when he was trussed up in the back of the wagon leaving New York. This time, however, he was master of himself. His blade cut and sprang in the water. Two ripples like black threads ran out from the prow across the ice-white surface of the stream. The tree trunks flickered by unbelievably fast on both banks: time seemed to have become something quite different. It might appear like this, Robert thought, to a bird soaring, to a trout darting along a channel. He felt winged and tireless.

He had no way of knowing how long he raced like this through the night, but he knew he had covered many miles before he stopped, balanced the paddle across the boat and drifted once more.

The air was cool, but he still felt warm and exhilarated

from the paddling. The silence and the stillness of the wilderness drew in about him as he sat there in the boat. That day he had worked for twelve hours in the cornfield; he had watched the Indians attack; he had been through surprise, horror and fear; he had probably killed a man; he had escaped in a stolen canoe and paddled as hard as he could for perhaps an hour. His body was exhausted, but it was a pleasant exhaustion. His mind refused to think of anything at that moment; it seemed to drift as the boat was drifting now on the strong, unheard, unseen current beneath. There was not a sound, not an owl hooting, not a splash. There was nothing to be seen except the full moon riding the sky and the dark trees slipping away on either side. Gradually Robert's chin sunk to his chest.

He awoke to hear the measured beat of paddles. There was a thick morning mist over the creek, but he could see that the canoe had drifted onto a shoal and stuck fast. All around him were yellow reeds.

He was alert in a second, listening intently. The sound was close and coming closer. The war party had caught up while he slept.

Perhaps the mist and the reeds would hide him. He looked about; but as if to mock his hope, he noticed that the mist was beginning to draw off.

Robert got out of the canoe into the water, making as little sound as possible, though he felt stiff and his movements were awkward. He walked a few yards, then glanced back at the canoe. The shape was all too obvious; he would have to find some other hiding place and quickly.

Taking the short hoe in his hand, he went off through the shallows, trying not to splash as he walked. The sound of paddling was very much closer.

He came out of the water onto a sandy beach. It would give his footprints away, but there was no time to worry about this. Once he was on firm ground, he ran. At the forest's edge he ran up hard against the bushes, then came out of the woods again to where a big pine tree stood alone. The tree appeared to have a branch about eight feet off the ground. After a rough climb he scrambled up and worked his way along the branch. Tufts of pine needles spread out thickly from the bough, giving good cover, but already the mist had thinned so much he could make out the tops of the trees on the opposite bank of the stream. As he looked down he saw a patch of water clearing, and into this came a black shape, long and low, like a snake holding its head up to strike. Ominous and fast the first canoe came on.

The figures in the canoe were blurred like mere phantoms, but when one of them coughed, the Indian might have been at Robert's side. He cowered down, hugging the branch.

As the first canoe pulled out of sight, he saw the bow of the second break through the mist. At that moment there was a loud flurry beneath him and two swamp birds broke cover. The noise was so startling and sudden that Robert slipped off the branch. He just managed to catch himself as he went, hooking one leg over and clutching with both hands, but the hoe had clattered down, he had made a noise falling, and the branch was waving up and down. He was quite sure he had given himself away. Whatever happened, he dared not let go. He remained there hanging upside down. Now the continuing noise of the paddling gave him some comfort; he only wondered how many canoes would pass. His hands hurt on the hard bark, and all he wanted to do was to drop off.

He heard voices.

There were at least two men talking. Robert heard them splashing about among the reeds, where he was sure they must have found the canoe. He tried to look around to see where they were, but it was impossible. He heard the speakers come closer still, and his heart beat wildly. They would find the hoe, look up, and see him hanging. In this position he was absolutely helpless. With what strength he still had he drew himself up tight against the branch. Pine needles tickled his neck and ears; his knees ached against the bark; he was sweating freely. He closed his eyes and prayed.

Long minutes passed. All the time, coming and going, came the voices of the Indians. At times they appeared to be just below his back, so that they could simply reach up and touch him. It seemed as though his last strength was about to go—another minute and he would fall off; but he held on.

Then he missed the sound of talking. He could hear no splashing and no paddling, no noise at all. He let his legs go, then his hands, and he fell heavily to the ground. Here he lay exhausted, hardly listening or caring what happened. Let them find him and kill him quickly.

He stayed where he was for half an hour or more. The sun came up. The last of the mists curled away. He was lying on a small promontory, which covered the roots of the pine tree and jutted out into the stream. On two sides he was screened by bushes and brambles, and on the other two sides the reeds blocked his view of the water.

It grew warmer. A bird started up from one of the brambles, singing "chick-chickadee-chickadee-phoebe-phoebe." A chipmunk came out of the woods, climbed up onto the handle of the hoe at the base of the pine tree, stared at Robert and scrubbed its face with its forepaws.

Robert watched the little animal and the chipmunk kept an eye, suspicious but curious, upon him. After a while, because he remained quite still, the chipmunk sallied out to within a few inches of Robert's outstretched hand. Here he began to chatter to himself, took a short sidestep, like an athlete preparing, then scuttled clean over Robert's hand and ran off chattering loudly, as though calling on the whole woods to acknowledge his courage.

Soon afterward Robert turned over and crawled, very slowly and without making a sound, to the edge of the bank. Once there he raised his head an inch at a time and peered out. Through a gap in the reeds he made out the form of the canoe. It surprised him to see it. He was sure the war party had found it, and yet they had left it behind. If he waited for an hour or two he would be able to get in and paddle on. There was no chance of his catching them up. They must be miles away now; they had missed him; he was safe!

And still he hesitated before showing himself. Instead, he crawled even more carefully to a wider gap in the reeds and lay watching the canoe and the stream.

Nothing was bothering the wildlife of the forest. Two ducks were floating a few yards from the boat. The birds were singing. A reed warbler went from reed to reed, clinging sideways with its little feet to the stem of each, singing a snatch of song, then darting off to another—a peaceful autumn morning in the wilderness.

In spite of this Robert waited. He never took his eyes off the canoe. Nothing happened. Time went slowly by and he was still on guard. Then, just as he was on the point of getting up, there was a splash. It was very faint, no louder than the sound Robert had heard a hundred times while fishing, the "plop" that told him there were trout about and that one had just risen to take an insect. Probably it was no more than this now. And yet it seemed to be the very noise he had been waiting for, instinctively, all that time.

When he next glanced along the canoe he noticed three or four bumps along one side. It was a good distance away, and the bumps were small, but it came to him suddenly that they might be the knuckles of a hand. Immediately his imagination pictured the Indian on the far side of the canoe, crouched down in the water, as he himself had waited on the previous night a moment before he brought the hoe crashing down on the head of the guard.

If there was one Indian hiding, waiting for him to break cover, how many more might there be? Every patch of the scene around him might contain a warrior, showing nothing more of himself than a row of bumps on the outline of a canoe. Yet each such clue could mean someone who was prepared to wait for hours, without moving, even in a cold stream, just for a chance to kill him.

If the Indians were able to do all this in order to kill him, he thought, he could do better to save himself from them. He remembered how he had blundered about before, how little endurance he had shown on the branch, how little he had cared what happened when he fell to the ground. "I'll outlast them," he whispered firmly to himself. "Let the savages stay all day in the freezing water if they want to."

And so, for hours on end, Robert watched and waited. Time and again he told himself that he was a fool, that the row of tiny bumps were obviously not knuckles at all, that he could remember them plainly as warp marks, then as rings of twine or rawhide. Anyone could see that was what they were! It was only his own stupid imagination that kept him there lying tensely, uncomfortably, all day long, while the Indians paddled on a good four or five hours' distance away. The sun beat down on his back. The flies and insects annoyed him. His hands hurt where he had scraped them. But he never moved. The sun climbed to its full height and started over. It was three or four in the afternoon. Then, quite suddenly, they were there in front of him.

He hardly heard the whistle from the woods nearby, when not one but two figures rose up from behind the canoe. They were big men, naked except for leather breechcloths. Their hair stood up in a black ridge, and the head was shaved on both sides of this. Two or three feathers hung in a bedraggled fashion from the scalp lock. One of the warriors had something tucked into his belt, and the long black hair, now wet, hung down to his knees.

There was something uncanny about seeing his hunters so closely after the hours of waiting. It was so unreal, Robert had an almost detached feeling, as though some game were over and he was safe now whatever he did. For five or six hours these were the three men who had concentrated on nothing else but killing him. Now they gathered together in a group by the bow of the canoe. He could see their fierce features, hooked noses, deep-set, almost invisible eyes and high cheekbones. Their faces had been painted with long slashes of blue and red. There were great daubs of red like fresh blood on their shoulders, and something like a bird had been painted on their chests. The two who had been in the water carried tomahawks; the man from the forest had a flintlock.

Now, as he watched, two of the savages climbed into the canoe. The third man pushed the boat off the shoal, swung it around and got in. They took up their paddles, pulled away hard and were gone.

Robert slept that night deep in the woods, in a grove of pine trees so dense that it was dark inside even in daytime. But his hours in the woods had taught him that he could wander, lost, in circles for days, finding nothing to eat but some hazelnuts and no way out. He tried to trace the way he had come and was glad when he saw the glitter of water between the trees. For all its danger, the creek was the obvious highway, the one thread through the maze. But there was no way of following it along the bank; he would need a boat of some sort.

Close to the place where he had come out of the forest there was a ledge of rock that jutted out into the stream. Against this ledge a large pile of driftwood had collected. Robert examined this carefully. Among the tangle he found a number of logs which had been stripped of their branches. The ends had obviously been cut by no axe, and he would have been mystified if he had not seen the beavers building their dam across a tributary of the creek near the cabin earlier in the year. He pulled the logs free and matched five of them. The whole day was spent in trying to bind these together with ropes of creeper from the forest. The result was disappointing: the logs were still very loose and the raft looked like a large, untidy nest floating on the water. For all that, it did float.

To make it more comfortable Robert brought branches and reeds and wove these through the strands of creeper. When this was done the raft appeared a good deal more tightly bound together. He had a springy mattress, too, to lie on, but it was more difficult to stand up and pole the craft along.

In the late afternoon he set out on his trial run. Below the ledge, and protected by it from the current, there was a still pool of dark blue water. Here Robert poled the raft back and forth. It went a little better than he had expected, but he was still doubtful whether it would carry him in the current.

An hour afterward the sun went down and the moon came out. The whole sky appeared to be alive with movement. When Robert looked at the moon he could see objects flickering across it like a school of minnows. They must be birds, he thought, thousands upon thousands of them, flying silently, except for the whirring of their wings, and flying at night.

In the morning he set off on the raft. All day he used the pole to keep the craft close to the bank. Often he clutched at the branches of trees or bushes on the bank to prevent himself from being drawn into the current. Most of the time he progressed at a much slower rate than he would have done walking if there had been a path along the bank. But all the time he traveled he remained on the alert for any sign of Indians. He stopped and ate hazelnuts whenever he came to them, but his stomach was tired of this diet and he had begun to feel lightheaded.

At dusk he pushed the raft into midstream, drew in the pole, lay on his stomach in the tangle of branches and let the current take him. Once again the woods opened up swiftly on either side to allow him through. From midstream, too, he could see all the colors in the lowering light—the evergreens, hemlock, spruce and pine, were somber black like great logs in a fireplace against which the foliage of the ash, maple, birch, sumac and oak licked and swirled with flames of yellow and every shade of red.

Something hurried along the shore among the roots of the trees. Ducks flew up from a clump of reed. A form was standing upright and still in a foot of water. For a moment Robert grew tense, thinking it must be a man waiting there. Then, just as he came to it, it soared up, a bird of almost pure white plumage with wings that could have been six feet in breadth from one black wing tip to the other. As it passed close by Robert could feel the vibration of the heavy wing-beat.

With the light going and the blue evening haze coming on, the fiery colors on both sides of the stream diminished slowly into banks of glowing embers. Then, when he could barely make out the outlines of the trees, he passed a wide gap on one side of the river. The current carried him very close to the low, marshy shore. Here one large form loomed up in the half-light. Robert had taken it for a tree, its strange shape accounted for by its having been struck and splintered by lightning. Then he realized with a shock that it was alive, a huge animal with great spreading horns. He could hear the sound of its heavy breathing quite distinctly now. He was very close and still the animal did not move. Robert held his own breath; he could almost have reached across the narrow gulf of water and touched one of the beast's legs. Again, it was like passing in front of the Indians on the mound. Something appeared to cast a spell on everything that came to the edge of the stream. Men and beasts, they stood there gazing out at the water as though whatever passed on the stream itself remained invisible to them.

On the next day Robert set about finding food, knowing he would be too weak soon to continue if he kept to fresh water and a few handfuls of nuts a day. He wasted several hours in the morning stalking wild ducks with his hoe, but they flew easily away from him. Then he stretched out by a pool in the rocks hoping to catch a trout by tickling it into his grasp, as he had heard fish were caught by poachers. But no trout came close enough to the edge. It made it worse to see them, brown shapes and shadows, a few yards away in the stream.

Abandoning this, he went to the woods and cut a long pole. He knew it was no use giving a fish spear a simple point, and so he split one end back for about six inches. Then he slipped a strand of creeper between the two split halves and bound this strand as firmly as he could to the shaft just below the end of the split. After this it only remained to shape the two prongs. The hoe was a clumsy instrument for doing this, and, in the end, Robert found it easier to sharpen the points simply by rubbing them on the stone. It was mid-morning before the fish spear was ready for a trial, and by that time Robert felt dizzy with hunger.

He carried the spear to the end of a rock promontory and stood waiting. Almost immediately a good-sized rainbow trout came nosing along, its form clear against a light background of sand. Robert brought the spear up, then plunged it in. There was a wild flurry in the water, but he knew without looking that he had missed the fish. Disgusted with himself, he moved to another place.

This time it was some while before another target presented itself. When it did so it was a smaller trout than the first and almost perfectly concealed against pebbles. Robert waited a whole minute watching the fish and then drove the spear hard where his eyes were still fixed. At once he knew by the feel of things that the fish was his. To make sure, he drove the prongs harder, forcing the trout against the stones. Then he brought the pole up and there was the fish wriggling in the sunlight above him, scattering down bright drops of water from the stream over his head and shoulders.

Robert killed it and laid it on the warm rock shelf, where the colors faded quickly.

He brought kindling and dead moss and built his fire in a

hole in the rock, weaving the fuel like a nest. He made sure everything he used was dry; he wanted no smoke in the sky to give him away. Afterward he took a gnarled section of pine, as dry as the hank of old rope it resembled, and another dry twig and then began to roll the twig between his palms, rubbing it against the piece of pine. Robert had never tried to light a fire in this way before. Nothing seemed to be happening. Whole minutes went by and his arms ached. Perhaps he had forgotten something very simple. He thought about the flint-and-tinder box lying somewhere among the charred ruins of Calvin's cabin. Perhaps he would have to eat the fish raw after all. But still he persevered. He was feeling angry with frustration and both his arms ached painfully when the piece of pine grew black and a coil of the moss turned a bright red. He went on—a whole minute longer, trying to forget the pain. The moss began to smolder and catch. A piece of tinder caught and flared up. Robert stopped rubbing for a split-second and added more fuel—too much! Had he put it out after all that? No, it was still going. He rubbed and blew gently and in a few minutes he had his fire.

There was nothing he could remember to compare with the taste of the fish when he had cooked it, washed it down with the cold water of the stream and eaten handfuls of nuts to follow it. He kept his fire going and hunted fish all afternoon, lying on the warm shelf of rock, driving the spear in whenever a fish came close enough.

By evening he had five more trout. He cooked them all, ate two and kept the other three for the next day. That night he drew the raft up under the trees and slept on it, covering himself with more branches and pine needles. He was full for the first time in days and he felt pleased too that he could make his way now through the wilderness like an Indian.

The next day and in the days that followed, he traveled on. Every morning early and every evening as the dusk drew on he would launch the raft into the current. In the half-light he felt far safer, but in broad daylight he would hug the shores, keeping the raft against the bank with the pole, peering ahead for any sign of the Indians.

He had been on his own for more than a week. The attack, his life with Calvin and Agatha, even the Indians lying in wait for him already seemed many months behind him.

Once more it was just at dusk. The raft was riding the current in midstream. He had come to dread the nights, when the cold woke him long before dawn to shiver and walk about for hours until it was light enough to launch the raft. He decided he would let the raft drift that night, and when it became too cold to sleep he would use the pole and keep himself warm with the exercise. It would soon be too cold to go on like this; each night was worse than the last. What would he do when winter really began? There was still no sign of Fort Charles. In six days he had seen nothing of any other human life but his own. Yet, just for that evening he was content to lie there on the brushwood and watch the woods go by. He searched the banks on both sides for animals. That morning he had watched hundreds of hawks flying back and forth in front of a great bluff of stone that rose from the side of the creek as if it existed simply to give them a background for their soaring flight. At noon he had brought down a duck by throwing the hoe at it. He was full now and warm. Again he watched the brilliant reds and yellows glow and fade out into blue, then black. The stars came out in the sky and again in the water. If it had not been for the cold at night, he thought, and for the Indians, he would have been content to go on like this month after month. He had never in his life seen anything more beautiful than this land, and it did not seem to matter just then that there was no one to share his feelings. Only he wished the Newt could have seen this. Then, all at once, a great wave of sadness came over him. Yes, he thought, if only the Newt could have been there to see it—just the two of them.

12

A Row of Blue Beads

IN THE MIDDLE OF THE NIGHT Robert woke with a start. It was too dark to see anything, but he had been awakened by a loud crashing and splintering of wood. Water, icy cold, flooded the raft.

Robert had no idea what was happening. He could feel the raft underneath him pitch and buckle as though the logs were alive, fighting against one another or trying to toss him off their backs. A second later he was jolted sideways where he hung with one leg now in the water. He tried to scramble back on. As he did so, the raft veered suddenly the other way, struck something, and, with a tearing noise, broke up.

The water seemed to take Robert as though it had been waiting for him. He felt the cold shock, felt himself being carried along quickly, then pulled under. His feet touched bottom; then he bobbed up to the surface. Something battered into him, thumping him all along his right side from his heel to his shoulder. Again he was ducked just as if someone had caught him by the ankles and pulled him down. He came up, struggling frantically for air, to be buffeted, twisted about and dragged under once more. This time when he came up he was scarcely conscious.

He found he was being swept beside what seemed to be a low shelf of rock. He put out one hand and his fingers ran along the surface above waterline as the current pulled him. The shelf flattened out just as his fingers tangled with something. Robert made a grab. He pitted all his strength against the current, brought his other hand over and got a second grip on what felt like a tangle of branches.

Now that he had stopped moving with it the current attacked him from all sides. His legs had swung violently around, but he still had the grip with his hands and he held on. His head was above water and he could breathe.

Robert wasted no time. He dragged himself back against the current until his elbows were bent and he was well up over the branches. Once there he jerked one knee up and managed to swing his foot onto the rock. When he found it was quite clear of the water he fought.

He fought like a fish fights against the line, threshing wildly, working in sudden lunges and spurts against the pull of the current. Once he had struggled up almost free of the water when he slipped on the wet stone and fell back. Instantly the current pulled him out full-length again and he had to start all over once more. He kicked and fought back inch by inch, got his leg up, then his side, then his other leg. At last he was out, hanging over the flowing water. Then he inched the upper part of his body down the branches onto the rock. He let his grip go, then rolled away over the shelf.

After he had stopped rolling he lay, face upward, gulping at the air as a stranded fish drowns in it. His hands were raw and bleeding. The muscles across his back and shoulders hurt as though he had torn every one of them. His legs were numb—but he was alive; he was out of the stream.

If he stayed where he was he knew he would not be alive for very long. He would have to move soon, before his limbs refused altogether. He sat up. The pain shot across his back and almost choked him. He tried to keep his arms and legs moving. Several times he had to stop because of the pain, but he drove himself to try again. In the end he managed to scramble to his feet. He walked forward very slowly and stiffly into the darkness ahead. He could hear the roaring of the water at his back, and the only idea he had of direction was to keep going away from the sound. After a few steps he felt moss, soft and springy under his feet. His hands touched the bark of a tree. He leaned against the tree and tried to rest.

It grew bitterly cold. What must have been far more than an hour went by. Somewhere a bird fluttered and then started to sing, but he was not yet able to see even the outline of the nearest trees. Robert rubbed himself from time to time. He walked away from the tree and came back to it. He knew if he once sat down and fell asleep he would die.

At last, long after he had given up hope, it grew slowly lighter; he could see his hands now, so raw he could hardly open them. His leather breeches were split to his knees on both legs and dark with blood. His sleeves were in rags.

The first gold rays of sunlight came threading through the trunks of the trees. With the sunlight all the warmth of living seemed to come back. He took a few faltering paces forward onto the ledge of rock. The whole creek to the far shore, ten yards away, was a race of churning white water. Farther downstream a few black rocks stood up above the surface. Against these the water pitched itself, cascaded and broke. A fine spray lifted in the air. As the sunlight grew stronger, colors, purple, orange and green, shown together like partly formed rainbows.

Beside the creek ran what, to Robert, looked like a man-made path. He started to walk along this, moving slowly and stiffly at first and using the trees on both sides to help him. When he came on the stump of a tree, obviously cut off by an axe, he wondered whether Indians or white settlers had cleared the way. He stopped for a while to look at the stump. It was the first real evidence of man he had come upon in many days.

Half a mile or so along the path, Robert arrived at an inlet where the fury of the rapids eddied out. Here he found what was left of the raft, two of the beaver-marked logs and a tangle of creeper. Hanging among the strands of creeper, its blade glittering in the morning sunlight, was the short hoe.

For a moment or two Robert stood undecided, looking at the wreckage, wondering whether to try to rebuild the raft.

Then he realized that it was hopeless. It would take him several days to find the strength to do the work and, for the first time, a path seemed to offer some way out of the wilderness. He took the hoe and went on.

After a mile or so Robert noticed that the trees were thinning out. A little farther on, he stepped out of the woods altogether and found himself on the edge of a broad meadow. Here he stopped and looked about.

The stream appeared to curve around in a broad arc. He could see it gleaming, straight ahead of him, perhaps half a mile away, across a flat field of grass. Another mile beyond that the forest began again. Farther off in the distance there was a range of mountains.

As soon as Robert left the trees he felt unprotected, open to attack on all sides, and he very nearly turned and hurried back to the familiar cover. He stopped often and looked about. At first, there was nothing to be seen.

He had almost reached the riverbank once more and he was walking without making a sound, the lush grass up to his ankles, when he came abruptly upon an Indian lying stretched out full length watching the stream. Robert stopped and froze still. But the Indian had heard nothing; he continued to look down at the water. Robert clenched the short hoe tightly in his hand and gazed down at the spot on the back of the savage's neck where the hair started to grow. It was at this moment that he noticed the row of blue beads.

At that minute, too, the Indian turned, saw Robert and sprang to his feet. Robert rushed forward and the two of them grappled at the edge of the bank, thrusting and pushing, their arms locked, Robert still gripping the hoe.

Inches apart they each gazed into the other's face. At almost the same time they recognized each other and released their grips. They each took a pace backward and stood, undecided, watching each other closely.

"Haieee," the Indian boy said, smiling cautiously for the first time. Robert smiled back.

The Indian came closer and put his arm around Robert's neck as he had done the night when Robert had set him free at Fort Charles.

"Good friend, you come again; my good friend," he said. He looked at Robert with his dark, sharp eyes, tapped him on both his torn knees and on his arms and clucked his tongue in sympathy. "Come," he said. "You can come."

The Indian boy kept his arm looped affectionately around Robert's neck.

They had not gone more than a few hundred yards when Robert noticed a group of mounds against a screen of trees. Out of the top of one of these came a strand of smoke. At first Robert thought these must be large ovens; then he realized they were houses.

"Good friend, very good friend," the Indian boy kept saying. But Robert was troubled with other thoughts by now. He had once rescued this boy beside him; nothing could change that. But for all this, Robert had seen too much of the savages since that night at Fort Charles.

He could hardly break away now and run; it was too late. He felt feverish, his thinking seemed blurred and his limbs ached; he was weak with hunger. The days were growing colder and he would die in the woods, that night or the next, left on his own. There would be food in the village ahead, warm fires, people sitting around them talking and laughing. But they were not his people. They were the same race—perhaps the very same Indians—who had attacked the cabin, who had murdered Calvin and Agatha, who had stalked him all that long day in the wilderness. Perhaps even this arm around his neck, this gesture which looked so friendly, was simply to make sure he came—to make a prisoner of him, in fact. The friendly words might be as suspect as the bird-taker's, leading him into another, worse trap. Robert stared hard at the huts ahead, as though he could tell just from gazing at the outside of them whether he would be looked after here or tortured horribly to death.

∾ 13 ∾

A Warrior Is Made

As THEY APPROACHED THE VILLAGE a tall figure dressed in whole skins the color of autumn leaves came out to meet them. The Indian boy slipped his arm from around Robert's neck and motioned him to stop where he was. He himself went forward a few yards and spoke to the warrior.

Although he could understand nothing of what was being said, some of Robert's first fears were dispelled; from the tone of his voice the other boy was obviously speaking on Robert's behalf. At least he was not being betrayed.

He turned to look at the warrior to see what effect his friend's words were having. At first he could tell nothing. The man's face was as lined as a section of bark, and it looked just as unreceptive to emotion. For some time he stared at Robert with a long, steady gaze from almost hidden eyes; then he said something to the boy.

The Indian boy began speaking again. At once Robert sensed the urgency in his voice. He realized that his own life or death was being decided on at that moment and that the balance had grown very fine. The warrior glanced back at him. Robert lifted his chin and returned a stare as hard and proud and indifferent as the Indian's. The warrior put out his hand.

The gesture was so unexpected it took Robert completely by surprise. The hand had come jabbing forward, the arm quite stiff, the whole movement more threatening than friendly. It was a second or two before Robert recovered himself and put his hand into the Indian's. He found the grip as firm and as wooden as he had expected. The warrior nodded to him, turned, and walked back, leaving the two boys standing together.

"Come—good!" Robert's friend said when he had gone. His eyes showed plainly enough how anxious he had been over the last few minutes. "You must come to my house, yes?" the Indian said and he led the way to the nearest of the longhouses.

His first experiences were all friendly enough. His rescuer, He-Who-Has-Killed-A-Bear, led him by the hand into the longhouse. It was a large building, three or four times the size of either of the cabins Calvin Moore had built. A whole row of young birch trees had been bent over into great hoops and on this framework the longhouse had been constructed. Seen from inside, it was like being under a giant gardening basket turned upside down. The walls and the roof were woven of broad strips of bark. In the center a fire pit was marked out with stones, with a hole in the roof above to let out the smoke. The fire pit itself was about four feet below the level of the ground and from it the earth was tiered, giving a series of earth benches, seats and couches. These were strewn with the skins of deer and moose and the thick robes of bearskin.

On that first afternoon, dazed with his fever, Robert hardly realized what was happening. He met a fat woman and a thin woman. Later he came to know them as his friend's grandmother, Black Swan, and his mother, I-Smile-Though-I-Am-In-Mourning. For the moment, the fat, older woman hurried off and brought him a wooden bowl full of stew. In his haste to eat Robert burned his mouth and swore. The old woman's face, which was so wrinkled and brown it looked like a patch of mud dried up in summer, cracked into even more and deeper wrinkles. She rocked back and forth with laughter. *"Tu est bon garc', tu est bon garc',"* she said, delighted with him. Afterward she sat watching him eat, chuckling to herself from time to time, rocking herself back and forth and sucking her lips in over her toothless gums.

The second woman, with a face as unlined as a girl's, came and felt Robert's brow. When he had finished the soup they gave him a handful of sharp-tasting black powder to lick. An hour later they had taken his clothes, wrapped him in a bearskin and set him on a ledge close to the fire. He slept, burning as though on fire all night, and woke to his strange surroundings in the morning feeling well again.

In a sense he soon became familiar with this life. He lived as the others did. Yet he realized in a while that the chief's family were protecting him from the rest of the tribe. He was not free to walk on his own through the village or to join the hunting parties. Outside the longhouse he met only hostile stares from the other Indians. He knew too that the family talked about him at night as they sat about the fire. Once when he stood by the doorway a shower of hot coals was thrown at him by someone who ducked away before he could see who it was. Fortunately whoever it was had thrown from too far away and the only damage he suffered was a burn mark on his sleeve. He thought that was the end of the matter, but Black Swan, too, had seen his narrow escape from where she sat working inside the longhouse. At the time she said nothing, but that evening she began, in a mixture of French and English, to tell him how bad the times were, how bad for everyone. Each man's hand was raised against the other, she said; there was no trust anywhere. It was not enough now to be the friend of the chief's son; he was still a stranger and an enemy. Did he understand? Robert nodded. "You must become one of us or one day they will find a way to kill you." She looked at him very steadily with her tiny black eyes and repeated herself: "You must become one of us. There is no other way."

To Robert it appeared to make little enough difference.

He needed no one to tell him now that his life was in danger, and so he nodded. He would do whatever they wanted him to do.

The old woman seemed a little surprised and put out by his straightforward acceptance. She asked again if he was willing to become a member of the tribe, and again Robert nodded. A few minutes later Robert saw her tell He-Who-Has-Killed-A-Bear what he had decided. His friend gave him much the same look as his grandmother had done, nodded at her gravely and went out.

What was done was done on the next afternoon. There was no sign of preparation, no warning, and Robert never realized while it was happening that he had freely chosen this as part of his formal adoption by the tribe. He was getting ready to go hunting when three warriors, bare to the waist, fully armed and slashed with warpaint like streaks of blood, rushed into the longhouse, seized him and dragged him out. All the women and children were gathered along the street of the village, to scream at him and to throw refuse as he and the warriors passed. The savages beside him howled; the dogs yapped and bit at his heels. Out into the meadow they dragged him. Here, every warrior in the village appeared to be drawn up in one of two long lines. Though he hardly recognized him in his warpaint, the row of blue beads around the neck of the first warrior in the left-hand file gave him away as his friend, now waving a club in the air and screaming at him just as savagely as the others.

The three warriors who held him tore off the patches and rags that remained of his shirt and trousers. They stamped them underfoot, danced around him, spat in his face, pulled his hair back and slashed it off in handfuls. Someone daubed him all over with a substance black as pitch and evil-smelling, slapping it over his chest, his face, even into his eyes. Half blinded, he was dragged by the arms to the head of the long files. Here they held him still for a minute. Then—agonizing! —he felt a flame searing his back. His hands were free; he leaped forward. As he did so the first two warriors struck him, both at the same time. "Run!" someone shouted in English. And he ran.

Blows crashed down on his head, on his shoulders, on his back, but for a hundred yards or so he kept his feet. After this he was tripped and he fell heavily. A warrior threw sand in his eyes, but he scrambled up, somehow, onto his feet. Now he put his head down and drove, wild with fury and despair, straight at the nearest Indian. His head struck the man full in the stomach. They went over together into the grass, but Robert had lost consciousness.

When he recovered he was lying wrapped in furs by the fire in the longhouse. It was nighttime and dark except for the flickering of the firelight. I-Smile-Though-I-Am-In-Mourning was squatting beside Robert watching him. Behind her, cross-legged and crooning to herself as she rocked back and forth, was Black Swan. Where had the two women been, Robert wondered bitterly, when he had been dragged through the village to the meadow? Noticing his eyes were open, I-Smile-Though-I-Am-In-Mourning held up a bowl to his lips and helped him to drink.

His head ached and he felt dizzy. He could remember every detail—every blow, it seemed—of his run between the files of warriors. He needed no one to tell him there were bruises all over his back, his head, his neck and the back of his legs. It was as though he had gone over the rapids a second time. His ribs ached even when he turned and lay on his stomach. There was a cold draft too on the top of his head. When he put his hand to it he found out why this was. All his long hair had gone. In its place there was one ridge of hair which stood straight up from the nape of his neck to his forehead. On either side of this he could feel the tender skin of his scalp—covered with lumps, bruises and cuts—clean-shaven. Both his ears tingled and his nose felt numb. Something had dried, too, like mud, in streaks across his cheeks. At first he thought it was the mess they had smeared on his face, but when he found it left a red mark on his fingers—war-paint! On top of this he was quite bare under the skins except for a breechcloth of soft buckskin. There was something, too, hanging around his neck on a string. He took this out of the covers to look at it and found it was a dark green stone, not much larger than his thumbnail. On one side, small, but quite clear, the outline of a porcupine had been scratched.

Black Swan had been watching him. "You are very brave, a brave warrior with many quills, Porcupine," the old woman said. But because Robert could not understand all her words, she pointed to the stone around his neck, put out her hand to him, then drew it back, mimicking the pain the sharp needles of the porcupine had given her so comically that Robert laughed outright. Now the old woman seemed to dance with the pain, her big body shaking all over, her face screwed up and her small eyes lost in a mass of wrinkles. Out of them, however, trickled tears of enjoyment as she gave herself over entirely to acting her part. "Oh woe! Woe!" she cried out now, flinging her hands up in pretended heroics. "Woe to the warrior who touches the porcupine!"

He-Who-Has-Killed-A-Bear came in and sat by his grandmother. He smiled somewhat shyly at Robert and Robert smiled back. All the same he wondered how many of the bruises on his back had come from his friend's club. He would have preferred to pretend nothing had happened, but it was the Indian boy who spoke of it. "Very good," he said in English. "I say you run, you run." Then the Indian boy chuckled with delight, remembering something. He turned to the women and spoke in his own language. At the same time he acted out Robert's run, his attempt to keep off the blows with his arms and his tumble. Then He-Who-Has-Killed-A-Bear did Robert scrambling up, choosing his warrior and then his head-butting of the man. He switched over to the astonished warrior. Back he went to the floor, all the breath knocked out of him by the blow in the middle of his stomach. The women roared with laughter.

Robert looked from one face to another. Perhaps it had been some rough practical joke after all, and yet it had been serious enough as far as he was concerned; the blows were real blows; he had been in no doubt at the time that he was fighting for his life. Nevertheless he laughed now with the others, though it hurt him a good deal to do so.

A Long Winter to the Coming of the Wild Geese

THOUGH HIS INITIATION into the tribe had been painful, it was at least complete. Robert met with no hostility now. Wherever he went in the village, braves who had looked as inhuman as the devils in old pictures when they dragged him out and beat him unconscious in the meadow now came up and solemnly embraced him. Even the oldest brought him a gift: a powder horn, bullets, moccasins, a string of charms against evil. The chief, Beak-of-the-Eagle, gave him an ancient French matchlock with a carved stock. It was heavy to carry and slow to load, but Robert found the gun reliable in firing and he soon became accurate with it in bringing down game.

The weather was becoming colder, and one morning the tribe awoke to find the river frozen over in front of the longhouses. It amazed Robert that he could go about wearing only his breechloth, leggings and a leather jacket. He often felt cold, but he was never really uncomfortable. It gave him a feeling of real freedom to be walking over the frosty grass of the meadow on a December morning with just these few loosely fitting clothes on him, taking only his gun, his powder and shot, and a little dried meat with him for the day's hunting. It amused him, too, to think sometimes of what he had become in a single year. What would Robert Entrick, the Squire's nephew, bundled up in a big sheepskin coat, riding from one fireside to another, have thought of this great lean savage with a shaven head and a scalplock who hunted all day long and slept at night rolled up in a skin on the earth like an animal in its burrow?

Often in the long evenings now Black Swan would teach him the language of the tribe or he would listen for hours on end to the discussions of the men by the fire. Hardly a night went by without a group of the warriors calling on the chief, and Robert fell asleep more often than not to the sound of their voices. At other times every warrior in the tribe was called for a conference. Then Robert took his place by the chief's son and did his best to concentrate on what was being said. After a few such nights he realized that the same question was being discussed on each occasion—what should the tribe do in the war that was raging in the wilderness? Should it join in the attack on the English settlements? Should it make peace with the English and defend itself against the anger of the French? Or should it send back evasive answers to both sides and do its best to remain neutral? Gradually, as his knowledge of the language grew better and by studying both the face and gesture of each speaker and the way his speech was received, Robert found he could distinguish those who favored each of the three possible courses of action and how much influence they had on the others. Once he had had difficulty in remaining awake in the drowsy atmosphere as the pipe passed back and forth. Now when he realized what was at stake and could understand most of what was said, Robert listened intently. However, he was wise enough not to take any part himself. One thing was clear: though the matter had been argued many times over, nothing as yet had been decided.

Usually Robert hunted with He-Who-Has-Killed-A-Bear. On one expedition, far from the village, his friend showed him the cave on the side of a mountain where he had won his name. They stood at the entrance looking in while the Indian told him how he and the bear had met head-on in a gorge below the cave, too close to each other for the boy to shoot, and how He-Who-Has-Killed-A-Bear had succeeded in clubbing the animal to death with his rifle. When Robert asked him whether there was likely to be another bear in the cave now, the Indian looked at him mischievously. "They sleep," he said, and he picked up a large stone. "Shall I wake one for you to fight, Porcupine?"

Robert said nothing, hoping he could bluff the boy out, and in the end he put down the stone with a laugh. "No good doing that. There would then be two He-Who-Has-Killed-A-Bears in the tribe. Who would know which one to call?"

They climbed higher up the mountain and came out on a windswept dome of rock at the top. From here they could see far out in all directions—the lakes, the hills and the forests. There was a great white sheet of water a few miles in front. From this a river ran out and coiled about until it ran into broad meadows. The village was hidden, behind a bluff, but Robert knew where it would be. He gazed out over the view, fitting into what he saw everything he had come across on hunting expeditions and during his weeks in the wilderness. In five minutes, standing on the mountaintop, he learned more about the lie of the land than in all those months of trying to find his way through the maze below.

As they were standing there an eagle sailed majestically over their heads. Without thinking what he was doing, Robert raised his gun to his shoulder and took aim. He was about to fire when He-Who-Has-Killed-A-Bear grabbed his arm and pulled the aim down. "No!" he whispered urgently to Robert. "He is our father, the father of the tribe—Chiunosi, we call him—he who watches the passes for us." And the Indian walked a step or two away and held out his arms to the eagle, which still circled the rock in slow circles. "Great Father!" He-Who-Has-Killed-A-Bear called out. "Take no offense at my brother. Go your way and seek out every enemy for us from your high place!

"He is the spirit of my grandfather also," the Indian said as they scrambled down the slope together on the way home. "If you had killed him, Porcupine, you would have broken the thread of our tribe—my father and his father and all our fathers right back to the beginning."

"Will you become an eagle yourself?" Robert asked.

"If I become chief. But only my spirit," He-Who-Has-Killed-A-Bear said quietly. "I would forget what I had been, but I would fly and keep watch over the tribe—the tribe of all my sons."

"Do people always forget?" Robert asked.

He-Who-Has-Killed-A-Bear frowned, thinking: "I don't know that, Porcupine. He knows—the eagle. Maybe Black Swan knows. But I think we forget."

He turned and looked back at the speck of the bird in the sky. "Yes, we forget, I think, but the thread of the tribe is not broken. To break the thread is worse than a thousand deaths —this I know."

Although he felt he was a true member of the tribe now, there were many things that still disturbed Robert. Something always seemed to come between him and those he was living with, often at just those moments when he felt most at one with them. He had forgotten, or at least forgiven, the beating he had received in the meadow (now three months behind him), but the scalps that hung from the center-post of the longhouse were always there in front of his eyes. He accepted the almost wild dogs that roamed the village; he accepted the sickly smell of offal that hung over the village even on a cold day, and he accepted, easily enough, the dirt and any discomfort there was—for the last there was compensation enough. But almost every day there were incidents in the village that repelled him—a woman crippled in a fit of anger by her husband, a child savaged by the dogs, a wrestling match between braves in which one man's neck was broken. Each time something like this happened he found he wanted to be off on his own for a while; he did not even want the company of He-Who-Has-Killed-A-Bear until he had had sufficient time to recover himself. Once, when he carried a child with a broken ankle some distance and tried to bind her foot, he was told sternly that such things were a job for women. It altered nothing in what he thought himself. It only reminded him of something he had once read: "A Man's Manhood is tested in time by many things, not least in his Mercy." Then he remembered that he had found it written in the flyleaf of a book his father had once given him. After this, though he joined with the tribe in everything they did, he kept a greater part of himself than usual to himself.

Meanwhile, with the heavy snows the hunting grew more difficult. They went in larger parties and searched farther afield, along the shores of the big lake, up the rivers and deep into the forests. Sometimes they built rough shelters and stayed away from the village for several days. The women went off too, far into the woods to tap the sap of the sugar maples. Even so the tribe often went hungry.

At last, when it seemed the winter would last forever, the hard frost broke, patches of earth appeared, catkins grew yellow by the river, and the birds and animals returned in such numbers Robert wondered where they had hidden during the months of cold. The men repaired their canoes for the time when the ice would melt. Already it cracked and broke in the lake with a sound that could be heard in the village.

Soon after this the thaw began in earnest. The whole forest seemed to be running with freshets of water. Unlike England, where the spring might last for as much as three months, here it was over in less than a fortnight. There was hardly any time between the melting of the last patch of snow and the first really warm day.

It was on such a day in the beginning of May that Robert returned from a hunting expedition of his own. He had been by canoe to the marshes on the other side of the lake, and the bottom of the canoe was full of duck and marsh birds he had shot. He beached the boat, strung the birds together, took his gun and started toward the longhouse. It was quite late and a damp mist was rising from the meadow, the aftermath of a thunderstorm in the afternoon. The sky was still red with the storm, and the red light reflected in the standing water.

Not far from the longhouse Robert made out two figures in the mist. For a moment he wondered what it was about them which had attracted his attention. Then he realized that it was the silhouette of their clothes: they were dressed like Europeans. From a distance of a hundred yards he heard a voice speaking—in English.

"So, it's worth a chance, don't you think now? There are supposed to be thirty or forty of them."

A sudden shock of delight came to Robert. He was about to rush forward and make himself known to the men when some instinct held him back. Instead he walked slowly toward them.

"It's not a lot for the trouble, that's what I'm saying," the other man said.

For no reason he could think of, Robert's thoughts had been carried back in an instant to a place he had not thought of in months, the hold of *The Charming Betty;* then he knew what it was: the accent of both the speakers was the same as that of the newcomers who had boarded the ship at Cork. The two men were Irish.

"And what do you know about such things—eh? Why, with forty of the right fellows Joncaire could take Albany, even New York itself." The other man laughed. "All right." The first man sounded aggrieved. "Don't we need every savage we can get?" Just then the second speaker noticed Robert approaching. He cautioned his companion to be quiet. Then, in a language close enough to the one the tribe spoke for Robert to be able to understand, he called out a greeting, followed by a request for him to take the two of them to his chief. Robert studied them carefully. They were both thin, bony men, dressed in clothes of a russet brown that looked too big for them and that had seen a good deal of wilderness travel. One of them wore the white cross-straps of a soldier and had a sword at his side. The other carried a soldier's pack, while a pair of ancient epaulettes hung by a few threads from the shoulders of his brown coat. It was as though each had borrowed something to give himself at least the beginnings of a military appearance.

The older of the two, the man wearing the sword, was now holding something out for Robert to take. As he took it Robert came close to thanking the giver in English, but again something checked him. He turned the coin over in his hand and found it was a French five-centime piece.

"Go and fetch your chief now, there's a good lad," the first speaker said, and the second translated it. But there was now no need for Robert to act: Beak-of-the-Eagle and two of the braves with their rifles at the ready veered up through the mists and stood facing the strangers.

"We bring gifts, gifts," the older man said quickly when he saw the Indians.

"Do you come from the English?" one of the braves asked.

"From the English? When did the English give you anything but fever? We come from your father, Onontio, in the north. We bring greetings from Joncaire, your friend. We come in the name of peace."

Beak-of-the-Eagle looked at them for a while before speaking. "Come then, I know you. I have heard of you before, the English-who-are-not-English. Whatever you say we must hear," he said. "Come, no one will harm you here. We will take your gifts and tonight we will talk."

The longhouse was full. The tobacco smoke was already thick in the hot atmosphere. Robert and He-Who-Has-Killed-A-Bear sat a little to the side away from the press of warriors but where they could see most of those facing them. By the chief the two Irishmen were sitting, looking uncomfortable at having sat cross-legged for several hours. Every warrior who wanted to had made a speech of welcome, and into his speech he had put his reasons for rejecting or seeking an alliance with the French. The older warriors were reserving themselves, waiting until the young men had finished. So much palaver, Robert thought, when will the real arguing begin?

Beak-of-the-Eagle turned to his uncle, Bright Dawn. The old man took the pipe and puffed at it twice. Usually he sat to speak, but this time he got to his feet and stood looking at them all silently for a moment. "I see twenty-two warriors," he said at last. "I see twenty-two and once there were a hundred. I, in my own time, remember a hundred warriors." He stopped and looked at them in silence. Nothing broke that silence until he coughed and spoke again. "Once we had as many longhouses as the Oneidas, as many longhouses as the Mohawks, as the Caynagas. Yes, in that day even the mighty Senecas treated us as one wildcat treats another, as the bear treats his brother. How many longhouses have we now, nephew?" He coughed rhetorically once more, expecting no answer. "What foolishness these young braves speak. Should the tribe follow these English-who-are-not-English on the scalp trail? What is to be gained? Does the falcon hunt with the eagle? What is to be gained, I say?"

"The price of an English scalp is a Louis d'or or forty bullets, old man," the man with the sword said.

Bright Dawn ignored him, sucking in his lips with displeasure at being interrupted. "What have we had in these last years from Onontio in the north? Fever, the Spirit that breathes the red spots of death through the longhouses; we have had men who shame our women, men like these who make promises, men who talk of the father's rights over his children. Yes, and from Corlaer, the English, we have had the same fever, the same promises, the same foolish talk of the father and his children."

"The English have armed the Mohawks of Albany and made them rich," Beak-of-the-Eagle said.

"So you said, nephew, so you said last winter and you sent your son, He-Who-Has-Killed-A-Bear, to treat with the English," Bright Dawn answered. "I know nothing of the rich Mohawks of Albany. I think this is another English story. But where are the Senecas now whose hunting grounds were from all the lakes to the great river? They too were friends of the English and now they have crossed over into the far lands on the other side of the great river; in all their old hunting grounds the English build their own longhouses. No, I say we were born free. We depend neither on Onontio nor on Corlaer. I say let us wait until the eagle brings down the eagle and the sky is safe once more for the falcon to hunt in."

The old warrior sat down and for some time no one rose to reply. Then a brave from the far side of the longhouse called out, "Let the man from Joncaire say again how much an English scalp is worth to Joncaire."

"A Louis d'or or forty bullets," the swordsman repeated.

"All scalps, even those of the women?"

"All scalps."

"But the scalps of the women and children are more honorable, more difficult to get. It has always been so. Joncaire knows this," the brave said. "To get such scalps one must get inside the longhouses of the enemy."

The two men in brown conferred together.

"You are right. Joncaire knows this. There are ten bullets more for such scalps."

The Indian gave a grunt of satisfaction, but did not speak further.

Half an hour afterward the conference had broken up. The warriors left the longhouse and the two visitors lay down on deerskin rugs spread near the door. Once again nothing had been decided for all the hours of talking. Tomorrow and, if necessary, the day after they would meet again to discuss the matter.

Robert tried to sleep, but it was hot and stuffy; the mosquitoes bothered him and he was worried. He lay for an hour or more wondering what the final decision of the tribe would be and what action he should take. He had been on the point of speaking more than once that night but had realized that he would give himself away without gaining anything. For the moment, however, it seemed that Bright Dawn had been successful in persuading the tribe to remain neutral.

Robert fell into a fitful sleep. He had one nightmare after another. In the first the town of Dorchester was attacked by strange Indians. He was just in time to rush into the Butterfield cabin as it caught fire and to rescue the young Butterfields. But when he brought them safely back to the village he was accused of treachery and ordered to run the gauntlet once more. After this the nightmares became less realistic and still more horrifying. From each he woke up running with perspiration to hear the steady breathing about him in the longhouse and the thin whine of the mosquitoes.

Just before dawn, he awoke for perhaps the fourth time and heard someone moving about not far from where he lay. The opening of the longhouse already showed paler than the walls, and against this Robert saw the silhouette of a brave. As he watched, two other figures joined the figure at the door. For a moment they merged together, then all three disappeared. Without a second's hesitation Robert got up from his deerskin and followed them.

The village street appeared to be full of moving figures,

but it was still too dark to identify those who were about.
Robert attached himself to two warriors, following a few
steps behind them as they moved out of the village and
through the meadow to the riverside, where the canoes were
drawn up on a shelf of sand. Here he squatted down with the
others gathered among the dark shapes of the boats. Looking
about him, Robert counted seven men besides himself. They
were still too indistinct for him to tell who was there, but
when one of the men spoke up softly, addressing the others,
Robert recognized the voice of the Irishman with a sword.
"Good now. You know the way, all of you, along the west
shore of the lake to the river at the other end. Up the river to
the second portage. Then you move into the great belt of
pine until you strike the military road ten miles above Fort
Charles. The English soldiers will come along that road as
I've said. Joncaire and the French officers with the other
Indians will be there at the bluff below Owl Mountain and
overlooking the road. If we get separated, go on your own to
the bluff, but don't be seen by the English—or by anyone
else, for that matter, especially when you come near the
bluff. When you're challenged give the word 'Onontio' and
paint a white patch on your chest—do you hear?—as soon as
you can. No Indian without a white patch will be paid by
Joncaire. Let's be off then."

Under cover of one of the canoes, Robert crawled quickly
away from the group and then looked back to see what was
happening. Three canoes were launched. In the back of two
of them Robert was sure he could make out the distinctive
silhouettes of the two white men. The Indians pulled away
quickly but with hardly a sound. In no more than a moment
Robert had the May morning to himself.

It took him very little time to come to a decision. There
was no point in returning to the village to make his good-
byes; they would be far too difficult anyway. If he simply
disappeared now in this way they would think surely he had
not gone by choice, especially as his gun was still lying beside

his deerskin in the longhouse. Probably his friends would suspect that he had been taken along by force with the war party against the English.

He walked along the shore until he came to his own canoe where he had beached it on the previous evening. The sky was lighter now, and as he paddled out into the stream Robert could see the shapes of the longhouses against the wall of the forest. He had a moment of regret at leaving. But the last doubt and feeling of indecision had gone. The tribe that had adopted him had broken up of its own free will; he owed it no loyalty. It was his duty now to go as quickly as he could to warn his own people against the ambush that was waiting for them at the bluff.

❧ 15 ❧

Ambush

HE HAD BEEN PADDLING HARD for five hours. The sun shone glaring on the water. Out in the lake to his left several rocky islands seemed to be suspended in the shimmering haze. Above them was the faint blue outline of the mountains. On the other side he was passing a coastline of high stone palisades. Large caverns looked out darkly from the rockface, their ledges full of birds. Below them were coves with beaches of gray pebble. Boulders stood out from the shore, the patches of red and green moss on their sides reflecting a second time in the still water.

Near noon he beached the canoe in a cove and bathed in the lake that had been fed so recently from the melting snow. After this he stretched out on a rock, drying in the sun and watching a great tangle of snakes in the shadow under another rock. Soon, however, he remembered the urgency of what he had to do, and he set off again with quick, steady strokes, hoping to put himself ahead of the others.

In the afternoon the dragonflies came out in their hundreds, skimming the water. The smell of the pine woods became almost oppressively heavy. Time seemed to have slowed to a stop, and the canoe scarcely appeared to be moving against the bank for all his hard paddling. At last a breeze sprang up in the late afternoon, but it was not until dusk that he came to the far end of the lake and found the entrance to the river that flowed out of it. By now he was exhausted, and the lush river meadows tempted him to stop

here for the night. The camping place looked a little too
obvious, however, and the same sense of urgency drove him
on. He turned the canoe around a spit of rock and into the
dark, pine-shadowed reaches of the stream. The midges rose
in swarms from the banks where the bushes grew thick over
the water, and wild ducks rushed back and forth in the
shallows with a great beating of wings, as though he had
alarmed them. He would have liked to stop and hunt one
down, but he hurried on. He traveled for several miles, most
of them in darkness, before he found a quiet pool among
pine trees protected from the current. Here he moored the
canoe to a branch and stretched out in the bottom. In spite of
the mosquitoes he was soon fast asleep.

He awoke with the first light and paddled on downstream.
Halfway through the morning he came to the first portage.
Here he carried the canoe on his head and shoulders along a
path that led through the woods. As he walked he could hear
the roar of the rapids through the trees, reminding him of
the struggle he had had on that October night to save himself
from drowning.

By mid-afternoon he had reached the second portage. Here
he hid the canoe among thick bushes and set off on foot along
a well-worn trail.

The sun went down and the moon came up. Robert was
still moving quietly and easily through the forest at a steady,
loping pace. Some time in the early part of the night he came
to a broad clearing. Here he took one side, careful to keep
out of the moonlight and in the cover of the trees. At the far
side of the clearing there were two oddly square silhouettes
against the sky. A sudden neighing made a weird and abrupt
end to the stillness of the night. Robert stopped and peered
ahead. He had almost run into a circle of wagons.

He got down flat on the grass and crawled carefully forward. In a little while he had spied out the encampment.
The drivers were asleep under the wagons. One guard, posted
on the far side of the circle, was awake, but the guard on the

side from which Robert had approached was fast asleep, leaning his back against the wheel of a wagon, his mouth open, his gun on the ground two feet away from him.

The next thing was to find out whether the encampment was French or English. Robert examined the sleeping guard carefully. But although the moonlight shone fully upon him, he was not in uniform and there was nothing in his nondescript appearance to tell Robert what he wanted to know. His narrow escape from giving himself away to the Irishmen had made him doubly cautious.

He felt a certain wry enjoyment too in looking down at the man as he lay breathing peacefully in sleep. Very quietly Robert removed the musket from where it lay and took it for himself. Then he picked one of the feathers out of his scalplock and began to tickle the sleeping guard under the nose. The man blinked a little, brushed the feather away and then let out a violent sneeze. Even after this he went on sleeping calmly.

Robert put the barrel of the gun up against one of the buttons on the man's shirt. He blew hard in the guard's face. The guard's eyes opened wide. He made no further move. He just sat there gazing wide-eyed into Robert's face, obviously paralyzed with fear.

"I hope I'm not disturbing you," Robert whispered. "I thought I'd better warn you there are Indians about." The guard swallowed hard, but continued to stare straight ahead without any other movement. Robert was tempted to go on with his game, but he lowered the gun. "It's a dangerous night to sleep on," he whispered. "Are you English?"

"What?" the guard said aloud. "Oh, God, go away!"

"Who's there?" a voice challenged from the other side of the wagons. Some of the drivers were stirring.

"Indians!" the guard croaked out. "Indians everywhere!" Then he began to shake so hard he collapsed on his knees in front of Robert.

In a second there was pandemonium. Figures came scrambling up from under the wagons, clutching their muskets, pulling their clothes together, cursing and swearing. A horse went wild, adding to the confusion by kicking the side of the wagon with its hoofs and letting out a series of piercing neighs like war-whoops. Someone started firing blind.

Astonished at what he had apparently started, Robert remained quite still. He was lucky not to be shot dead. Instead he found himself overpowered, knocked about and dragged here and there, until someone had the idea of making him fast to one of the wheels of the wagon. Though he protested in English, no one took any notice. Gradually calm was restored to the scene and the supposed Indian attack was over. Robert began to fear he was going to pay heavily for his game with the sleeping guard. He heard the man's voice boasting now. "Well, we got one, didn't we?"

"How many were there?" one of the drivers asked.

"You saw them yourself," the guard returned cautiously and cleverly. "You saw them yourself. Oh, we'll find a few bodies out there in the bushes tomorrow, I warrant."

They shouted loudly back and forth in excited voices. An iron bucket clattered; someone dropped a gun. There was enough noise in the corner of the clearing to alert any Indians for miles around.

The guard came up to Robert and put the point of a skinning knife against his chin. "We'll deal with you in the morning, my buck."

"Listen to me," Robert said as quietly and as distinctly as he could. "Will you take me to an officer? I've got an important message for him."

"What officer and what message?" a wagoner asked, overhearing his words and approaching. Then without waiting for an answer he started to search Robert. Something slipped out of his clothes and glittered in the moonlight. The guard bent down and picked it up. He examined it and whistled. Robert realized they had found the French coin the Irishman had given him. What on earth had possessed him to slip it away like this and then to forget about it!

"He's a spy!" the guard said with some awe. "What did I tell you! Speaks English too like the Lord Mayor. He's a rare one, this buck, with his French silver!"

"I can explain about the money, I promise you I can," Robert said. "But please trust me enough to take me to an officer. I've got news for him that can save us all from falling into an ambush."

The wagoner stroked his chin. "I don't know who you are or what you're doing, my boy," he said, "but since you don't appear to know the name of a single officer in our army and since you carry French coin and attack English sentries in the middle of the night I don't choose to believe your yarns." With this he walked off to return to his sleep, leaving a by-now wide-awake guard to sit beside Robert as he waited out the long hours until morning, sitting with his arms stretched out, tied to a wagon wheel. More than his discomfort, Robert cursed the waste of precious time and his own bad handling of the situation.

Early the next morning the camp broke up. When the wagons were drawn up in line to move off Robert was attached by a long rope lead to the last of them so that he could walk beside the team of horses.

Throughout the morning, in spite of the fact that the driver of the wagon often gave him a cut with the whip for doing so, Robert called out to be heard.

"That mad Indian!" one wagoner yelled over to another. "Tell that mad Indian to be quiet!"

"Is he paid by the Frenchies to frighten us with his talk of ambushes?" another shouted back.

"He'll be freighting trees soon enough," a third answered grimly. "Let him preach a whole Tyburn sermon over himself if he has a mind to. Let him cry out 'grammercy' to the man with spade and quicklime for want of six and eightpence for the chaplin's cut."

Robert tried again, first threatening them with what would happen, then pleading with them to be sensible, to take him at least to one of the officers, but it was in vain.

The sun shone hot above the trees. Robert walked on mile after mile in the dust beside the horses. Early in the afternoon they came to a hill and everyone was called on to help the teams to get the wagons up the slope. While they were at work Robert heard something above the noises near at hand. It was music, music here in the wilderness! And it was coming closer.

They had no sooner reached the crest of the hill when an officer rode up on horseback and ordered the wagoners to make way for marching troops by drawing their wagons to the side of the military road. As soon as this was done the soldiers came in sight. Skirmish lines were moving on both sides of the road, glimpses of scarlet through the trees and undergrowth. Then up the hill in the center came the advance guard of the column. Directly behind the first company was the band, three files of side drummers and three of fifes. After this there appeared to be a small orchestra, various musicians playing an oboe, a bassoon, a serpent. There were even three fiddlers, also in scarlet with gold facings. And there was a Negro boy dressed entirely in white, clashing a set of cymbals together. On his shoulder, unworried by the noise, sat a monkey with a feather headdress like an Indian.

A group of officers had ridden up not far from where Robert was standing. Robert did his best to attract their attention, but his voice was drowned by the band. The music boomed and crashed and tinkled and oom-pahed as they passed him. To Robert's despair the knot of officers dispersed.

Now the main part of the column was passing, file on file in scarlet and white, a few files in bright buff-yellow with white leggings. As they passed they sang, a great rolling sound that gathered and flowed around the steady beat of their tread.

"Why, soldiers, why
Should we be melancholy, boys?
Why, soldiers, why?
Whose business 'tis to die.
What, sighing fie!
Damn fear, drink on, be jolly, boys!
'Tis he, you or I,
Cold, hot, wet or dry.
We're always bound to follow, boys,
And scorn to fly . . ."

The singing grew fainter. The column had gone over the crest of the hill. From where Robert stood he could see almost the entire length marching away downhill. It moved, twisting and straightening itself out again, like a single living thing, like a huge red serpent, its scarlet coloring a brilliant contrast to the green forest that filled the eye as far as the horizon.

But even as he looked, the forest seemed to swallow up the column into itself, the wilderness closing again as the last files disappeared into its vastness. Now the music of the band and the singing grew fainter, until there was only the steady vibration of the marching feet.

Late in the afternoon came another sound, the noise of battle. As soon as the firing started the wagoners drew their wagons into a circle and armed themselves.

Some time went by. The firing continued, but it was otherwise still. Once a light breeze blew for a few minutes, carrying the sound of firing closer, and with this the noise of drum rolls and the thin music of fifes. Again the stillness and heaviness of the afternoon closed down over the battle. To Robert, who waited out each minute with a hammering heart and an almost sickly feeling of anxiety, the wagoners appeared to show no concern at all. Several of them had taken out their long pipes for a smoke; others stood using their guns as props, talking to one another. He wished he were over there in the battle, instead of here in this odd, uncertain atmosphere of quiet.

This thought was interrupted by the sound of a horse galloping. A minute later the rider burst from cover below and came uphill as hard as he could ride. In his haste he almost ran into the circle of wagons. "Get away!" he screamed from his horse, seeing the group of wagoners. "Get away! They'll be here in a minute! They're finished, massacred to a man!"

He skirted the circle of wagons and rode on, telling them nothing more, but his words had thrown the whole scene into confusion. No one waited to discover who had been massacred or who would be there in a minute. Each wagoner cut loose a horse from one of the teams, leaped up into the saddle and rode off after the messenger. For a moment everything was commotion, shouting and cursing; then Robert found himself alone.

He was still tied up and secured to the wagon by the leash. Fortunately in his haste to be off one of the wagoners had dropped the knife he had used to cut the traces and free his horse. Robert could just reach this, and after a struggle he managed to cut himself loose of his bonds.

He was at liberty again at last, but what was he to do? He had no desire to follow the wagoners. Instead he set off at a run in the direction of the battle. He soon left the road, however, and took to the forest, keeping his eyes and ears on the alert all the while for the first sign of the Indians.

He had not had to go far when he heard the scalp cry, full and high and chilling. It grew louder and louder as Robert ran on toward it.

A mile or so farther on he came quite suddenly in sight of a section of the road. None of his fears for the column had prepared him for the sight that met his eyes. The whole stretch of the road that he could see between the trees seemed to be covered with bodies, unmistakable in their scarlet cloth. Along the road parties of braves raced back and forth. Some carried burning branches; others had scalp knives in their hands. As the party went by Robert caught sight of the white marks on their chests like the blaze mark on a tree. He remembered then what the Irishman had said during the conference among the canoes.

When he had an opportunity he scuttled down a bank and onto the road. Here he squatted down beside a dead soldier. By spitting on his fingers and working on the pipe-clayed cross-straps the soldier wore he was able to take enough of the white paste to counterfeit the white mark of the French Indians. Using blood, he gave himself warpaint. Then, disguised, he took the soldier's gun, powder horn and bag of shot and set off up the road.

Whenever other braves passed him Robert brandished his gun and let out the scalp cry, hoping, each time, that there was no one among the party from his own tribe who would recognize him under his thin pretense.

As he ran, it became all too obvious that the ambush had been a complete success in catching the column off balance and annihilating it. Now he noticed band instruments among the debris, a smashed fiddle, drums with their skins stoved in, one of the cymbals gleaming up in the sunlight. He wondered if even the monkey had escaped death.

He could hear scattered firing in the woods off the road. Perhaps isolated parties were still holding out there against the Indians. Near where the head of the column had been he ran into a party of braves dispatching the wounded. Sickened by what he saw, unable to do anything on his own to prevent what was happening, and hoping he might still be able to help some of the soldiers escape the same fate if he found them in the woods, Robert left the road, climbed a steep bank and plunged into the thick undergrowth of the forest. Here the Indians had waited for the column. From here they had fired at a few yards' range into the packed files, remaining almost unseen themselves, firing down and protected by loose boulders.

Even on the slope Robert came upon the bodies of several skirmishers. Each man had been separately stalked and killed with a knife. Again Robert noticed how conspicuous their uniforms made them among the tangle of bushes and fern.

So far he had not seen a single dead Indian.

He was thirty or so yards from the road, walking uphill, when a twig snapped in two to his left. Robert brought his gun to his shoulder as he spun around. Ten yards away a British officer stood watching him.

John Lawrence was unarmed. In the early part of the fight he had been struck on the head with the butt of a musket and he had only just regained consciousness. He still felt dizzy from the blow. Now he found himself alone, facing an Indian brave armed and splashed with fresh blood. There was little point at that range in trying to escape. He gazed with composure at the gun that was leveled at him and waited.

Uncertain what to do to shed his disguise without losing every advantage, Robert decided to keep treating the officer as a prisoner. "Walk on ahead of me up the hill," he said.

Farther from the road, they came upon a thicket with thick ferns and undergrowth, which would provide at least a temporary shelter. "Sit down," Robert said, "and listen to what I have to say."

If he was surprised by what Robert told him, the officer showed no sign of it. He listened, but Robert was certain he remained unconvinced, both that he was only in disguise and had tried to warn the column, not taken part in the attack on it, and, more important at that moment, that the column no longer existed, that they could do no more than save themselves. When Robert said they would go as quickly as possible from the scene of the battle, John Lawrence flatly refused. He insisted on staying to rally his men. Robert wondered whether to threaten or to bargain. He decided that threatening would have little effect.

In the end, when Robert had insisted that he take off his coat of scarlet and stoop down low in the underbrush like

himself, they made their way back to a position from which
they could look down through a gap in the foliage at a stretch
of the road. Bodies lay scattered several deep in places. None
of them moved. There was no sound now. The Indians had
gone elsewhere. Even the birds had stopped singing. There
was no one to rally here.

Even then John Lawrence insisted on waiting. He would
agree only to remain in hiding. Robert, thinking he under-
stood the officer's thoughts and his sense of duty, but knowing
they could do nothing useful now and what would happen if
they were discovered, was tempted to leave him. "Do you
want to be tortured to death?" he said bitterly. But he stayed.
And the officer, without answering, continued to stare down
at the road and the ranks of dead.

16

The Siege

DURING THE HOUR they had waited they had seen no one, heard nothing.

The late afternoon had turned the woods almost red. One of the wagons still smoldered on the road, and the wind blew the smoke up through the trees so that it looked as if the forest was on fire.

Robert got to his feet. "We must be off now," he said. "We'll try for Fort Charles. It's less than ten miles away, though we'll have to go through the woods, and that may add a bit to it. At least there's a stockade at the fort and supplies—that is, if the Indians aren't there before us." John Lawrence at last nodded agreement to his plan. He gave one more glance at the devastation on the road below. Then he appeared to shake something off and a second later he was on his feet ready to follow Robert.

They started at a good pace. Though the officer seemed very clumsy and noisy to Robert, he managed to keep up. Soon they passed through the place where the Indians must have camped. Sections of bark on some of the trees had been torn off and messages and threats had been cut into the bark, the letters blackened with soot. On one birch tree Robert recognized the marks of his own tribe.

They traveled on for several hours without speaking, stopping only once to drink from a stream in a valley.

After dark they had to move much more slowly, and it was a relief to Robert that at least the officer did not ask for time to rest. They pressed on for over an hour more through the thick woods, Robert keeping in mind the general direction of the military road, hoping his idea of the distance had been correct, and alert for the first sight or sound of Indians.

At last they came to a gap in the trees. Here, not half a mile away across a clearing, was the unmistakable silhouette of the fort. It was a starry night and a flag still flapped at the top of the flagpole—but which flag was it?

"We'd best wait for morning," Robert said. "Even if the English still hold the fort the guards will shoot at anything that shows itself." John Lawrence nodded agreement and slumped down against a tree stump. In spite of the cold of the night he was fast asleep in a few minutes. Robert left him where he lay, and in the two hours before he rejoined him he had crawled over a mile, reconnoitering all the ground around the fort. He was unable to discover who occupied the fort, but no one saw him or challenged him from the guard posts.

To their great relief the first light showed the red Cross of St. George on the white cross of St. Andrew flying above the fort. John Lawrence put on his uniform coat. Though one sleeve was now in ribbons and the cloth was covered in stains and burrs, he did his best to smarten himself up. Walking together, the two of them approached the stockade. At the sight of the scarlet coat the gate was opened at once. Robert entered Fort Charles for the second time in very different style from the first occasion.

In a matter of minutes the news traveled through the fort that the relief column was in sight. The same news died bitterly all too soon afterward.

There were forty-one men, twenty women and twelve children of various ages at Fort Charles. All the men were well armed and experienced with firearms, though some were still weak from an outbreak of fever which had decimated the settlement in the early spring. The same epidemic had brought it about that the leader of the community was now a tall, dark bearded fellow whom Robert had no difficulty in recognizing as Jacob, the man who had done his best to have him hanged the previous May.

From the moment he set foot inside the fort and looked around, John Lawrence had been all activity. Without discussing the matter he had assumed immediate command, ordering up lists of all able-bodied men, guard rosters and inventories of supplies; telling Jacob the number of guards were to be doubled forthwith, the gate must be closed and blocked with all available spare timber—the fort, in fact, was to be put on a siege basis as quickly as possible. The only thing the officer appeared to be doubtful about was what to do with his guide, Robert. He had noted the looks of suspicion Robert had been given. It was either a question of putting his former guide under close guard, or of trusting him completely. In the end, on evidence, he decided to trust him, which meant to accept every word of his story.

"If you're an Englishman, as you say you are, you'd better dress as one here," he said. They had reversed their roles of leader and follower, Robert noted wryly. In the forest the officer had accepted his every command without question; here it was he who was expected to obey. "Did you say your real name was Robert?"

"Yes," Robert said.

"Well then, Robert, thank you, you saved my life last night, even though I only half trusted you at best," John Lawrence said, and he held out his hand with a smile. Robert shook his hand and forgot his resentment. "You can help us here with your knowledge of the Indian ways," Lawrence said, "but you had better borrow some other clothes, don't you think, for your own safety?"

It was ironic, Robert thought, that the clothes he agreed to wear should come in the end from Jacob. It was odd too that these clothes came very near to fitting him, so much taller had he grown in a year. It felt strange to be clothed from head to foot once more; it was stranger still to be called

Robert after over a year—Robert Entrick, Jack Allen, Kestrel, Porcupine-With-Many-Quills—and now, finally, back to Robert again. It made him think nostalgically for a moment, for the first time in a long while, of Northumberland, of the Hall and his old life. If he was no nearer to returning to his home, at least he had won back his old name.

"Robert," John Lawrence was saying, "what do you think of our chances? Be honest with me. Those French-led Indians have already swallowed up a battalion of well-trained troops and the rough fellows here have had the wind knocked out of them by the news. Do you think there's any fight in them?"

"There will be," Robert answered grimly. "When they catch sight of the first Indian there'll be enough fear to sustain them fighting until they drop. No, I'm not worried about that. Everything depends now on the stockade and the supplies. If we managed to hold our own, when could we expect any help?"

"Help?" John Lawrence said. "You mean soldiers or colonial militia—it's doubtful, at least for a while. It will take a good many days for them to get the news, and they've lost almost every man they had to send out. No, we'll have to hold our own here for a long while. Besides, all the guns, the ammunition and the stores with the battalion will have gone to those Indians."

"Which means we've got nothing but a wall of green wood between us and an army that's drunk with its own success. Still, we might manage it if we make haste to prepare ourselves," Robert said. "Come, I'll show you something."

They walked around the walls of the stockade. On three sides it stood up between twelve and fourteen feet high, strong and firm. On the fourth side overlooking the river, the wall was still the line of six-foot-high palings which Robert had helped He-Who-Has-Killed-A-Bear to scale the year before. "Watch!" Robert said. He gave the wall a push and the logs moved over to an angle. "The wood's rotten here. We might as well be protected by paper. It's like having a good strong front door to a house and leaving all the windows wide open at the back."

"What can we do in the meantime, do you think?" John Lawrence asked.

"We might be able to do quite a lot," Robert said. "A victory like the one over the column will need celebrating." (He did not want to go into how it would be celebrated and that the time which was precious to them would be bought by the tormenting of prisoners.) "Leave this wall as it is and build another one twelve feet high, directly behind it. Then if we get caught in the middle of the work, we'll at least have something more than we had before to protect us."

Within a quarter of an hour everyone on guard was at work. A line of sentries, placed at regular intervals, protected the most direct route from the working party at the edge of the woods back to the stockade. Along this line men, women and children passed all day pushing or dragging the logs for the new wall as they were cut. The axemen worked in two teams, two men to each team. One of these teams was made up of Jacob and Robert.

Although Robert had no illusions about the man, he had to admit to himself that he had never seen anyone cut down a tree so quickly or so skilfully. A certain degree of comradeship grew up between them in the heat of the work, and Jacob grew friendly to the point of making jokes about how Robert now looked in his new clothes.

After several hours' work in the sun, however, both men were very nearly as bare as Indians, the sweat running freely on their bodies. All the time, above the strokes of their axes, they were listening for another sound, the first war whoop. But it did not come.

There was someone else besides Jacob at the fort who interested Robert, a small man who appeared to be carefully avoiding the working parties by changing his guard duties skilfully about. For one spell he would be on guard at the stockade, and the next he would stand sentry by those who were carrying logs. Something about his pinched, almost twisted face reminded Robert of someone he had once known. The man looked on the elderly side, but he was surely just as strong as some of the children and the young girls who were working so hard in the rush to finish the stockade in time.

Robert was debating with himself whether to say something when Jacob, as though reading his thoughts, paused for a moment and scrutinized the fellow. "Idle, whistling old jailbird," he said to himself and cursed. "You there," he called out. "Did you come all the way from England to lean on your musket and whistle while you watch us work? Give the women and children a hand with those logs or I'll scalp you smarter than any Indian." So saying, he swung his axe once around his head and let it go. It sailed up, then came down, and the head thumped into the ground about a yard from where the guard was standing. The guard quickly abandoned his place to one of those who had been working all day and threw himself with a great show of enthusiasm into helping to haul one of the logs to the fort. Jacob let out a roar of laughter, strolled over to retrieve his axe and then came back. "I hope the savages get that gray scalp. It's worth nothing to us," he said.

After a day's work felling trees, Robert spent most of the night on guard. The hours passed without disturbance, though he grew tense and listened more carefully whenever an owl hooted. Behind him he could see the logs of the new stockade. In a day they had built up almost half the wall.

All the next morning they worked with few interruptions in the hot sun. Then, late in the afternoon, the sky clouded over and there was a sudden heavy thunderstorm. To those who had been working, the rain, however heavy, came as a relief and they continued what they were doing, letting it run over their skin and drench their clothes. Soon one of the guards announced that there was a gap of no more than four feet to be filled; perhaps five more logs would be needed to fill it.

The downpour stopped. A party of women were dragging one of the logs back, their feet slipping on the wet ground, when a shot rang out. In a second the scene changed. Everyone scattered and ran for the shelter of the stockade. "Come on!" Jacob shouted back to Robert. "They're just over there, by the turn of the road!" Robert picked up the axe in one hand and broke into a full sprint. Jacob was well ahead of him by now, and Robert found himself the farthest from the fort, running across several hundred yards of open ground. The firing was frequent. The gate of the fort, he knew, would be closed. Only the gap at the back remained open and he sprinted for this. As he ran he came upon one of the women, who had tripped in her wet skirts and now lay flat on her face in the mud. When Robert caught her up under the arm to help her, she let out a frantic scream, imagining herself about to be scalped. Robert half dragged, half helped her around the side of the fort. The gap was still open and they were soon inside.

Every guard post of the fort was manned. John Lawrence hurried from one to the other giving orders and encouraging the men. There was little need for him to give the order for them to hold their fire; too many of them had allowed their powder to grow damp in the downpour.

"A hundred Indians and two or three Frenchmen," Robert said as he stood on the rampart close to the gatehouse beside John Lawrence. "That's what I'd estimate them at."

"Surely there are more than that!" John Lawrence answered. "I'm positive I've seen more."

"A hundred's quite bad enough. No, it's like trying to count a flock of birds; unless you're careful you get the same man turning up a dozen times as he doubles about through the brush from one firing position to another. There may not be as many as that—so far!"

"What are they doing now?" John Lawrence asked.

"Putting up effigies along the front of the woods to frighten us, all of them dressed up in the scarlet coats they took from the column."

"But some of those aren't effigies, they're bodies," John Lawrence said.

"Yes, some are." (Anyway we can't see them too well at this distance, which is a good thing, Robert thought.)

Someone in the woods blew a bugle and there was a parody of a drum roll to accompany it. Then a piece of white material was waved about on the end of a stick. "They want a parley," Robert said.

"Who, the Indians?" John Lawrence asked.

"No, there must be a Frenchman or two with them," Robert said. "Let me go out and see what terms they'll give."

Something of John Lawrence's old suspicion of Robert seemed to creep back into his expression. "But they aren't going to stick to terms, those people, are they?"

Robert gave a somewhat caustic smile. "Whether they will or not, I'll get a better look at them from there than from up here and, besides, we need the time for the powder to dry out. I give you my word I'll report whatever they say back to you." When the officer agreed, Robert suggested they drop him over the side of the stockade by rope so that the Indians would not be encouraged to rush the weak side of the fort. He advised John Lawrence to have the gap in the new wall barricaded up while he was away. As they were lowering him over the side, he suddenly remembered his head and shouted for someone to give him a hat. "If they see my scalplock, I certainly won't get back to you alive. And will you keep your guns on the man I'm talking to," he called out. "If anything happens to me shoot him down. Ten to one he'll be their leader."

At the foot of the stockade Robert scrambled out of the noose and started to walk out across the meadow. He had never in his life felt quite so much alone as he did in these moments in which he approached the knot of figures by the edge of the woods.

He recognized the man dressed in brown who came out a little way to meet him, but he was careful not to give away any hint of his recognition. The epaulettes, he noticed, still hung by a thread or two from each shoulder of the man's coat.

"Now what are we going to do, do you think?" the Irishman said in a friendly enough fashion. "I've three hundred savage fellows here screaming for blood from the lot of you and I'm doing all I can to restrain them. Will you make it easier for me, or must I let them do what they will with you?"

"What are your terms?" Robert asked.

"Terms? Why, the terms are simple enough—that you march off with all the honors of war and leave us your fort."

"But you say you can barely restrain your Indians," Robert reminded him.

"In a manner of speaking I can't and in a manner of speaking I can. It depends, don't you see, on the mood I'm in and the mood they're in. I grant you it's a risk, but it's certain death if you refuse."

"Not so certain," Robert said.

"You've a bit of wood out there, enough to keep the draft out, and perhaps fifty men all shaking so hard with fear and the fevers they'll bring the fort down by themselves. Did you hear about the relief column that was supposed to come to you?"

"I did," Robert said.

"It was a nice short battle."

"I know," Robert said. "I was there."

"Were you now?"

"Where's your friend, the one with the sword? I owe him fifty centimes," Robert said.

"Do you so," answered the Irishman, obviously thinking hard by this time. "Well, you'll not owe it to him long."

"I've had your terms. I'll take them back and discuss them with my Council of War," Robert said.

"Council of War! Four mice and a pheasant." The Irishman laughed out loud.

"How long have we got to decide—an hour?" Robert asked.

"It'll be dark in an hour. No, you've ten minutes. If the gate's not wide open by then we'll set fire to you. Have you any women and children in that fort?"

"Some," Robert said.

"Well, it'll make you think then, won't it?"

"It will," Robert said, "at a Louis d'or and ten bullets for each one of their scalps."

With this he turned on his heel and started back, trying to show no sign of hurry that might be mistaken for fear, though he could not forget how easy it would be for them to shoot him down as he walked.

17

Woe to Him Who Touches the Porcupine

TEN MINUTES LATER Robert was back at his observation post on the front wall of the stockade. The gate of the fort was still firmly closed.

"What will they do, do you think?" John Lawrence asked.

"They may try a fire raid this evening, but everything's wet after the storm. All the same we'd better have every bucket that can be found filled and ready."

He had no sooner spoken than the first fire arrow came humming up through the air. It crossed the line of logs and fell behind them into the fort. Within seconds they were coming in large numbers.

"Don't bother with them," Robert said. "Above all tell the guards to ignore them. The women should be watching where they fall from some protected place. If one looks as though it will start a bad fire, then she can go out and deal with it. If we have everyone rushing about trying to put each one out as it lands we'll lose a lot of people unnecessarily."

Jacob nodded and went off to give orders accordingly.

As dusk came, the inside of the fort began to resemble a foundry. Small fires burned among the rubbish heaps, throwing up the dark outlines of the walls and the cabins. Fire arrows streaked red over the black logs of the stockade and against the dark blue of the sky. Outside the Indians had gathered together all the branches the axemen had cleaned off the logs used for the new wall. These the Indians had sprinkled and daubed with pitch. They had carried them up to the walls of the fort and set fire to them.

Fortunately, as Robert had said, the heavy downpour in the afternoon had dampened everything so thoroughly that most of the effectiveness of the fire raid was lost. "Keep your eyes open and shoot if you catch the Indians outlined against the fires," Robert shouted out to the guards. "But make sure you're not shown up yourselves in the same way." He turned to John Lawrence. "They'll make at least one rush tonight, they're so confident," Robert said.

They had not long to wait. "Stand your ground," Robert shouted out, trying to get his words heard as the whole night was filled with the screaming of war whoops. "Stand your ground! Don't fire till you see a target. Club them if they come over the top!"

John Lawrence had been on a tour of the guard posts, encouraging each man in turn and making sure he had powder and shot. "This is your rush then," he said, coming up to Robert. "How do you think it looks?"

"Well, for one thing they've had no time to make scaling ladders. That will slow them up a bit, even though they'll use lopped trees. If we can get a cross-fire going early and watch that pocket of hidden ground on the right where they're almost bound to get ready for the final rush, it will help keep down the numbers of those who get to the stockade."

"Jacob," John Lawrence called out. "Get a few of the women up here to load. Keep the rest of them and the older children ready with buckets to deal with the fires and see the younger children are well out of the way. Tear down any rag or cloth you see and have any rubbish doused down. Above all keep them standing firm whatever happens."

The screaming grew louder. The men along the guard walk fired, reloaded and fired again. Then in a moment the Indians were there, swarming out of the darkness, up their improvised ladders and over the front wall of the stockade. Robert used his musket as a club and struck out, knocking one brave off into the night. Someone came running along the guard walk behind him, and Robert saw it was Jacob. In his hands he carried the axe he had worked with all day. This he now swung around and around his head, and he fell to clearing the guard walk of Indians in a frenzy of cold fury. One after another the warriors shied away from his path, some falling into the fort to be away from the axehead. Then one brave climbed onto the parapet again and leaped, knife in hand, upon Jacob. For a second the two of them hung there locked together; then, before Robert could reach Jacob, both men fell sideways into the fort.

Robert ran the length of the guard walk—the whole front wall of the fort was free of Indians! Those guards who were still alive were hurrying back to their posts. "They're going!" a man said, wild with joy as he passed Robert. "Fire at their backs!" Robert called out. "Kill every one you can; it's your one chance."

"Now then, Robert," John Lawrence said, "how goes it?" He stood there in the square leaning against the flagpole. His once-smart military coat was a wreck. His face was stained with blood and gunpowder. His hair stood all on end and his eyes were bright as sparks with the excitement of battle. "How goes it, Robert, my fellow-captain?"

"For the moment very well," Robert said. "We've pushed their first rush back. They'll think hard about that. They never like such things and they were very sure of victory. But how many have we lost?"

"I don't know," John Lawrence said. "Jacob's dead, which is bad. Four or five others, I should think, dead and wounded."

"More, I'm sure," Robert said. He himself had counted three guards killed on the front wall.

"Will they attack again tonight?" John Lawrence asked.

"I doubt it, not in the dark," Robert said, "but you won't get a lot of sleep."

And as Robert had expected they would, all through the night the Indians outside howled, fired their rifles, shouted insults and tried their best to terrorize the besieged into submission.

In the early morning they attacked again. This time they chose one of the flank walls and approached it silently in the half-light. The guards on that side must have been asleep. The first Robert knew of the danger was hearing a piercing shriek and seeing a guard fall backward into the square. It looked as though the whole guard walk on that side was crowded with Indians.

In the first moment of peril Robert was tempted to rush up one of the ladders and join battle hand to hand on the guard walk. But he noticed that even in this poor light the Indians made good targets with their backs to the inside of the log wall. He knelt in the square and fired. One of the braves toppled over. John Lawrence fired, so did several others. In a second or two the Indians were under a good rain of fire. As they came over the top, they were even more clearly outlined against the sky. Robert had already counted five or six braves killed.

"Keep firing!" Robert called out. He went himself to help in one of the hand-to-hand fights going on in two of the corners of the stockade. But then as he climbed the ladder and looked back he saw that every one of the guards who should have been standing sentry at the new wall in the rear of the fort had turned to fire into the fort against the Indians trapped on the flank wall. Just above the line of stakes Robert could see the river. Along it, silently and very fast, came a line of war canoes. Down the ladder he clambered, then raced to the rear of the fort. "Get back, you idiots!" he shouted. "Watch your own side!" He grabbed one man, spun him around and held him up to the stockade. The man caught sight of the convoy of canoes passing unimpeded along the stream. "Oh, my God," he said. "More!"

"Yes," Robert said, "more!"

They succeeded in freeing the fort of Indians, but the cost was high. The fighting force had been reduced to twenty-eight, including two women who could shoot. They had used up the best part of the powder and shot. Meanwhile the Indians had flanked them and established themselves on the weak side of the fort in a protected place under the bluff where they could not be dislodged by fire from the stockade. Whenever they chose to attack their approach would be hidden by bushes and the lie of the ground until the attackers were almost under the new wall.

For another thing, the day promised to be hot and without any likelihood of thunder or rain. If this were so it would be perfect weather for a fire raid by the evening. For all that, Robert was not entirely discouraged by the way things were going.

"Two attacks and we've beaten them both off," he said. "They've probably paid more already for our few scalps than for those of the whole column. Another unsuccessful attack and a good many of them will start drifting away of their own choice. The price of our heads is rising quickly in our favor."

"I'm glad to know it," John Lawrence said. "It's like fighting a lot of mediaeval devils—every time you fire at one he disappears, leaving nothing behind but a whiff of brimstone. Let's get everything ready for them next time. I don't want to go through many more of those moments."

So he said, but from the look on his face, Robert might have wondered if he enjoyed it.

The day passed without a shot being fired. No Indian showed himself. The inevitable optimists among the guards on duty started the rumor that the Indians had gone for good. Those not on duty picked out a place in the shadow and slept for the first time in two days. A heavy torpor settled on the fort. It worried Robert that the men could go back so quickly to thinking everything would be all right. There under the bluff, he knew, were perhaps twenty warriors who, if they chose their time well and made a determined enough attack, were quite capable of taking the fort on their own. They would have to think of some ways of defeating them, or, at least, of forcing them out of their present position. He was turning various plans over in his mind when the sound of whistling broke in on his thoughts. Not far from him, leaning against the stockade, the gray-haired guard who had angered Jacob the afternoon before for his laziness was whistling quietly to himself. Where have I seen him before? Robert wondered. He looked almost like an Indian, with his sunken, leathery cheeks, his small eyes, his mouth that seemed to be pinched in and his short gray hair. Then, as the man changed over to another tune, a strange feeling came to Robert. There was a quality in the whistling, almost a coaxing note he remembered well enough. For a moment he was transferred from the fort in the wilderness to a hilltop far away in Northumberland, to a winter's night, to almost pitch-darkness, and the sound of just such a compelling whistling. Even a little of that long-ago fear came to him, as though he had never outgrown it. He looked again at the gray-haired guard. There was no mistaking him. He wondered why he had taken so long to realize who he was. Was it because the Birdtaker looked older, less jaunty and less crafty, as though something had taken away his old certainty in his odd powers? For all this, Robert felt a trace of awe in being so close to him again; it was several minutes before he broke the spell.

" 'The World Turned Upside Down,' " Robert said.

"What's that, sir?" the man asked.

"The tune you were whistling—I know it, I've heard it before and I've heard you whistling it."

Nothing appeared to alter the Birdtaker's expression, but it was some while before he answered. "So you know me then, sir. I had a notion you'd remember your old friend. I saw you yesterday with that Jacob fellow that's dead now. I thought to myself, that's him, though he might not want to know an old friend now that his position's so changed. That's him, I thought, that's the lad who rode with me all that winter's day and whom I saved from the wrath of that mad animal, Ben Regworth. Yes, I knew you well enough, having made a study of such things, but you've changed. We've all changed, come to that. Still, it's something to come up with old friends again, especially in a predicament like this one."

For a moment Robert thought he had caught the ghost of the Birdtaker's old ironical self, and when he said "friends" for the second time Robert looked quickly, expecting to see the twisted smile he remembered so well which had shown the Birdtaker was having his own grim joke at someone else's expense. Instead he found an expression that was close to an appeal on the man's face while the corners of his mouth were turned well down.

Robert said nothing, therefore, and the Birdtaker, assuming all was now well, brightened a little. "Do you think we'll come out of this, the pair of us? You know the Indians better than most, I'm told. What would you say—odds-on chances?" Robert said nothing. "Worse then. I thought as much. I'd have done better to take my chance with the Justice, you know, at the Assizes than come here and roast on a spit."

But Robert had been thinking hard all the time he spoke. A plan, already half formed before in his mind, now, incredibly enough, seemed to have been given a chance of success— just a chance, but still a chance.

"No," Robert said, "I'd say it was somewhere near even, or *could* be."

"Would you put money on it though, sir?"

"I might," Robert said, "if I could get those twenty or so armed braves sitting under the bluff over there out of the way."

"Still there, are they?" the Birdtaker said.

"Still there," Robert repeated. "How good are you with that knife of yours nowadays?" Robert gestured to the curved knife which he remembered so well and which he saw still hung at the Birdtaker's side. The Birdtaker's eyes grew larger. Robert spoke again: "And could you make bird noises like you used to, to lure others into your hands? Could you teach me enough to imitate one bird well in an hour's teaching? If you could do all this, then I'd say there's a good wager in it."

"You've a plan, then?" The Birdtaker was wide awake now. Some of the old craftiness had come back into his eyes.

"I've a plan," Robert said. "Wake another guard to take your place and come with me to see the lieutenant.

"With two of us," Robert was saying, "there's a chance."

"It sounds pretty wild to me," John Lawrence said. "It's all based on what you *think* the Indians will do. You should know, of course, but why are you so sure their attack will be like this when it comes?"

"Because it worked so well for them this morning," Robert said. "While one party attacked a flank wall, this group was able to come around by canoe into position under the bluff and no one so much as shouted at them. Tonight it will probably start with a fire raid, then, when the fires are going nicely and we're at least half occupied with putting them out, the first rush will be made at the other flank wall. Almost every man will be needed to deal with this, but at that point the real attack will be made along the new wall."

John Lawrence looked concerned. "I agree it sounds like the worst sort of trouble we could deal with. When will it come?"

"At about dusk again," Robert said. "The fires will take about twenty minutes to start, and neither attack will begin until they see that parts of the fort are burning. If you can spare the two of us to deal with the party under the bluff, we'll do our best to cope with them."

"With twenty?"

"Twenty at the most and we'll be using a trick to trap them."

"And you want to take this man here?" John Lawrence said as though he felt dubious of Robert's choice.

"He's the only man I could use," Robert answered with a smile. "Oh, and we'll need a reliable guard at the gap in the new stockade, which I'll be using as a passage, someone who looks hard before firing. If anything goes wrong we may be shot dead on the way back."

"All right," John Lawrence said. "I hope you've guessed right. I don't like the idea of your being outside the fort at all, especially in the middle of a battle."

Late in the afternoon Robert and the Birdtaker began to prepare for their raid. They took off their clothes and wore nothing but breech cloths. A dead Indian provided one for the Birdtaker. Next Robert shaved the old man's head, giving him a scalplock like his own. After that he daubed them both with warpaint and put the white mark like a blaze on their chests. Armed, each of them, with only a knife, they crouched down beside the barricade of furniture that filled the gap in the new stockade and waited.

Half an hour afterward the first arrow came over. It stuck a cabin and the flame began to lick quickly up the wall toward the window. A child rushed forward from cover, doused the fire with a bucket of water and hurried back as more arrows came down. Robert had prepared two palliasses full of wet straw. As soon as the fire arrows began to come down he lit a dry patch of each of them, climbed to the guard walk and tossed the two burning bundles outside the fort to exactly the spot where he wanted them. Here, the wind blew the thick smoke across the gap and screened it from the bluff.

He scrambled down again. "Let's be off," he said to the Birdtaker. "Remember," he called out to the nearest guard, "make sure of the Indians you fire at from this direction tonight. We'll come in calling out the name of Lieutenant Lawrence."

They clambered up the pile of furniture and odd timber, then dropped onto the ground outside the fort. Here they got down among the tall hot grass and began crawling for the bushes and the river. Robert, knowing the ground, soon found a slight depression that would cover them for most of the way. It was the obvious route too for a party attacking the fort.

Two hundred yards on they stopped and put their heads together. "We've got to act like a couple of sheep dogs," Robert whispered. "Don't forget to drive them the way we want them. It won't be easy."

The Birdtaker looked at him and grinned his old smile at last. "It'll be lovely and bob-easy, like springing partridges, mark my words, no more trouble than that rabbit we had for our breakfast. It's a pretty rig you thought up, sir, one after my own heart."

"Good," Robert said, smiling himself in a somewhat forced fashion. "I'm glad you like it so well. But take a look at my feathers before you go off. Don't make a mistake about me in the bad light."

"Nor you neither," the Birdtaker muttered, his voice hardening for a moment in suspicion. Then he cheered. "What a game this will be! Who'd have thought I'd have changed myself into a savage." His eyes gleamed wickedly.

Choose a thief to catch a thief, Robert thought to himself. "Is there anything else that isn't clear?" he whispered.

"It's all clear, good luck and rum pickings, my buff," the Birdtaker whispered back, then he thought and went on: "I meant to harm you once, I'll own it, but we're friends, I hope, in this."

"We're friends in this all right," Robert answered. "I wish you luck too. Remember every one we get goes toward the score. If the score is high enough they'll get discouraged and leave us—it's as simple as that. This is our one good chance."

"Aye," the Birdtaker whispered. He gripped his knife and waved it at Robert.

Robert watched him back away quietly through the thick grass. What other man in the world would have been as good for the job in hand? Robert thought grimly.

Behind him the fire raid was at its height by the sound of war whoops and the crackle of flames. He did not look around. Instead he crawled quickly forward along the fold in the ground. Very soon he began to hear the sounds of something coming to meet him, the gobbling of a wild turkey. There were other sounds like it to Robert's right, but none to his left. By listening again, then crawling away, he worked his way to the flank of the attackers. Now from time to time he stopped and gave the same sound himself. He found too what he had been looking for, a group of rocks half covered with bushes. Here he made a gobbling sound once more and waited. It was only a matter of minutes before the gobbling of a wild turkey came out of the dusk no more than a few yards away. The brave was crawling along the edge of the defile. Robert waited for the man to come abreast of him, then he rose from the bushes, grabbed him by the arms, blocked his mouth and plunged in the knife. When it was all over he rolled the body into the defile, lay down, signaled again and waited.

It was nighttime now, but the fires in the fort lit the landscape with a lurid red glare. The whole fort appeared to be burning from the outside. Had it fallen? Shots rang out still and occasional war shoops, but the scalp cry had not gone up. Robert crawled up the defile as quickly as an animal, though he was impeded by three powder horns slung around his neck. There was no time for anything now but getting back to the fort. Ahead of him he could see the wall of the new stockade and the gap of the passage point. Everything so far had gone according to plan. Just in front of the fort an Indian lay slumped down. Robert would have given him no more than a glance, but he noticed the man's feathers and his gray hair. In a second he had rolled the Birdtaker over. He was still alive. Though he was covered in blood from his neck to his knees, only a little of it, from a shot in the chest near the white patch, was his own.

"Some fool fired as I shouted out 'Lieutenant Lawrence,' " the Birdtaker said. "Some fool shot me from the fort."

"All right," Robert said, "I'll get in and come back for you."

The Birdtaker's eyes hardened once more. "Will you, by Hell's fire!" he said. "I'll die as you wanted me to, sprung in your double trap."

"I'll be back," Robert said firmly.

Robert left him and approached the passage point cautiously. There was nothing for it. He started up, climbing over the broken furniture. But no one challenged him or fired. When he got to the top and looked over, he could see no one. All the guard points appeared to be abandoned. Robert pitched himself over and dropped inside.

"Who's there?" someone called out.

"Robert Entrick. Hold your fire!" he replied quickly, but he kept well out of the light. One sight of what he looked like at that moment would probably have been enough to start them shooting.

"We'd given you up, sir."

"Had you" Robert answered sourly. "And did you have anyone attack you over this side of the fort?"

"Not a soul, sir. They were all over on the other side where Lieutenant Lawrence was, thousands of them, but we pushed them back."

"Good," Robert said. "Then get me some clothes before I'm shot and a bucket of water. After that I want you to come and help me get someone in." The guard did what he was told though he showed some hesitation about going outside the fort. In the end he came.

18

An Old Tale Retold

THE ONLY CABIN that remained virtually undamaged by fire had been taken for a hospital. Even here there was no escaping the smell of burning from those parts of the fort that still smoldered. John Lawrence lay on a mattress on the floor. He had been climbing one of the ladders to the guard walk during the attack when part of the gatehouse had fallen in, bringing down the ladder and half burying the officer under burning timbers. He was trapped for some minutes before someone had rescued him and taken the weight off his legs. His hands and face were only slightly burned, but his legs were both burned and broken. He was in great pain now, and there was little that could be done to ease it.

Robert had brought in the wounded Birdtaker to find his friend and six others in a similar state with only two women to look after them. The beds and tables had been used for the barricade. The wounded lay on the floor, where they coughed with the smoke. The heat of the fires, added to the already-hot night, made conditions still worse. All Robert could do was to make the Birdtaker as comfortable as possible with a bed of loose straw. He helped the two women to stretch wet muslin over the open window frames. This kept out most of the insects, the smuts and some of the smoke. Then Robert came back to his friend and dampened his forehead with a wet rag.

"How did it go, then?" John Lawrence asked, managing to

lift himself up on one elbow. "Have we beaten them, do you think, Robert?"

"It's too early to tell, I'm afraid," Robert said. "We should know in the morning."

"Well, let's pray they've gone by then," John Lawrence said. "Lord, if they come in tomorrow they can walk over the fort. By my calculation there can't be more than fifteen men left standing. Still, for all that, it was a fine hot fight we gave them tonight. How did your plan work?"

"It succeeded," Robert said somewhat shortly; he had no wish to go into details. "By the way, we brought you back some powder and shot in case they're needed. The old man got hit by some fool of a guard firing when we came in."

"I was afraid of that happening." John Lawrence lay back again and stared up at the ceiling, bracing himself from time to time against the spasms of pain. "They've no discipline, no proper training, not even the sort of sense needed to be soldiers, these fellows. You can't make them hold their fire if they don't want to. Still, say what you will, no soldiers I've seen could have fought harder."

"It's amazing what courage and fight comes into a man when his scalp's in danger," Robert said sourly. "But how do you feel now?"

"Quite horrible," John Lawrence said. "Quite, quite horrible. Whenever I shut my eyes for a second I dream I'm being roasted alive by Indians. What have you done about the fort tonight?"

"Kept five of the men on guard for two hours, told the rest to sleep and take turn and turn about. I'll have them all up an hour before daylight," Robert said.

"Sir, oh, sir," someone called out. "Can't you keep the mosquitoes off us!"

"I'll go to him, Mister," one of the women said. She squatted down beside the man and fanned him with a handful of ancient yellow playing cards. "There's that old fellow you brought in wanting to speak to you, Mister," the woman said.

Robert moved carefully around the outstretched bodies on the floor to where the Birdtaker lay on the other side of John Lawrence.

"Ah, there you are," the Birdtaker said, seeing him. "And you *did* come back to fetch me out there, my buff."

"Don't be a fool," Robert said.

"But I never thought you would, you know. Still, it's no matter. We did well, the two of us out there in the long grass—eh? Not one got through that I could see—cut them off like Christmas geese," the old man cackled, then felt a stab of pain in his chest and coughed. Robert changed the subject quickly and asked him how he was. "Dying, of course," the Birdtaker said with a good deal of impatience. "Still, I'd say it was worth it, worth a lot it was, that last trick. Never saw one to better it. Besides, I'd have been turned off years ago at Newgate if I hadn't been fated to be killed out here. I can't complain much. They're all dead by the rope, my brothers, one sister and my father—before ever I came into this world, so I hear. Ben too—almost everyone I've known, in fact—and yet here I'm dying game of a soldier's wound, no less, won on the battlefield. That's something to read about." He gave it some thought, then realized he had been led away from his main purpose. "Listen," he said to Robert. "Before I die or go raving stupid I've a word to say to you. I've no love for you, but I owe you something and I pay my way in the world. I did you a bad turn and you paid me back with a good one. Aye, and for all our differences we were close enough in tonight's game to play fair with one another. You brought me in here off the roasting hook to die like a gentleman. Now I'll do fair by you. Do you remember Ben?"

"I do," Robert said.

"He was a drunken lout, but I tricked him, to speak plain and honest, I tricked him out of the money we had for you."

"From Captain Mask?" Robert asked.

"Mask? We had but thirty guineas from that tallow-faced captain. I thought you'd think that. No, the other, think hard, we had a hundred pounds from him."

"What other?" Robert said, but a suspicion was already nagging at him.

"Why, the fine gentleman in the fine house that sent for us all the way from London and treated us to his port and his views on politics."

"You don't mean my uncle, do you?" Robert said.

"Likely enough it was your uncle," the Birdtaker said. "He had the same name you have and lived in the same house. Wanted you out of the way quiet and no questions asked. Ben, now, was for killing you and burying you out on the heath, but I knew of this dodge of selling you for a bondsman and being garnished twice over. So you owe me your life in a manner of speaking, though I won't press the point. Still," the Birdtaker said, "to go on. I lost Ben quick as I could and came to London, where I lived quiet for a while, then somewhat loudly for as long as the coin lasted and then back to quiet again as it is in life. But Ben, like a fool, went up north to your uncle and said he'd been tricked and would need another hundred or he'd go to the nearest constable with the tale."

"Did he get the money?" Robert asked.

"He did. He set himself up for a fine gentleman. Drank an ale house dry and played host to half the tavern drunks of London for a week or two, but it never lasts. So, north he went again and came back with more, but this time someone had it away from him before he ever set a foot in London."

"You, I suppose," Robert said.

"Me? Wrong this time. But get me some water, sir. I can't talk with a mouth as dry as this." Robert brought him some water and helped him to drink it, though it started a fit of coughing and seemed to do little good. The Birdtaker lay still for a while afterward, licking his lips; then he spoke again. "No, I'd had no part in it, though I might have had if

I'd known. Still, he was sure it was me. He came after me, but I'd soon fixed him for good."

"Killed him?"

"No, if I *had* killed him I'd have been a lot safer and wiser. I shopped him, informed on him, got him put in Newgate on suspicion of robbery I knew he'd done a year or so back. But it did me no good in the long run."

"Why was that?" Robert asked.

"Well, as soon as he saw the walls of Newgate rise around him he thought I should be there too to share it with him."

"So he informed on the informer?"

"In a manner of speaking—yes. Only as luck would have it a flyer gave me the news they were out with a hue and cry for me, so I came away quick of my own free will to the Colonies."

"As I did by no choice of my own," Robert reflected out loud. "So it was my uncle who hired you both. Have you any evidence?"

"Evidence? Why no, your honor, none," said the Bird-taker. "You'd best go back yourself and ask him whether he did it or not." And with this he cackled until he choked. "Well, I've spoken out fair, told you who it was wanted you out of the way. Will you see I'm given a soldier's grave, not dumped in a pit of quicklime for want of six and ninepence like all those others—say, will you do it or not when I'm dead?" he asked very seriously.

"Don't worry, I promise I'll see it's done properly if you die," Robert said.

The grin returned as ugly as before.

"Who'd ever have thought I'd die so honorable?" the Birdtaker reflected gaily, then he laughed and brought on another more violent choking attack.

"Robert!" John Lawrence called out as he passed him. "Listen, I heard all he said to you and fitted it in myself to what you've told me before. If you're wise you'll write out what he said about your uncle's hiring him to put you out of the way and get him to sign it with the names of a pair of witnesses. Then if it ever came to court you'd have something to go on. If he dies both your witnesses are gone and it's your uncle's word against yours."

"I'll do it," Robert said, "and I'd better get it done soon. But it puzzles me why my uncle should do such a thing. As far as I know I'm not the heir to the Hall or to any great inheritance."

"Have you seen any deeds or your father's will?" John Lawrence asked.

"No," Robert said. "But I was told there was nothing much—a little money from my father when I was twenty-one, two hundred pounds or so."

"Who told you this?" John Lawrence said.

Robert thought hard, then gave a slow smile. "What a fool I am! Why, I remember it now. It was my uncle, Uncle Thomas Entrick himself, who said that."

⤜ 19 ⤛

Several Milestones Are Repassed

THE MORNING CAME. There was no attack. Robert had the few remaining guards standing to for an hour, but not an Indian showed himself.

"The cost of our scalps must have proved too high and they went where they thought there were cheaper ones to be had," Robert said to John Lawrence, hoping he would not have to take his words back.

An entire day without an attack seemed strange, almost purposeless. As soon as the emergency eased a little the air of torpor returned. The guards left their posts and slept where they could find shadow. No threat or order would stir them.

The day went by, a week went by. On the third day the Birdtaker died. Three more of the wounded followed him to the line of graves set along the new wall of the stockade—dug inside the fort because those that were left were still reluctant to venture out. The Birdtaker had had his last wish. Doing his best to keep the fort on some sort of military basis, John Lawrence had started an Orderly Book, and on the day the Birdtaker died the officer recorded that "John Crofts, Private, died this day of wounds." His name they had discovered from the written confession he had proved willing enough to sign for Robert two days before he died.

"Keep that carefully, Robert," John Lawrence said. "We'll

show it to my father when we reach London. He's an attorney and will be able to advise you what to do."

More than anything else, it pleased Robert to hear his friend so confident he would reach London. The poor man could not stand, and even sitting or lying were painful. He found some relief in trying to run the fort from where he sat among cushions in the square under a sunshade, his two legs strapped to splints sticking out in front of him.

By the end of the month there was little to remind them of their two-day battle for survival—the black burn marks on the wood and a few charred strands of timber, logs that had been pitted with shot, the row of graves, the bandages of dirty cloth worn by the wounded. The heaps of litter, rag and offal between the cabins had begun to fill up again—as Robert remarked caustically: "Ready for another fire raid to burn the place down once and for all."

"Sometimes I wonder," John Lawrence said, looking about, "how we ever managed to save ourselves."

On a morning in July the cry of "Redcoats coming" was heard from the guard above the gate. John Lawrence had barely time to prepare himself before the gate was opened and the column, splendid in scarlet and white, marched in.

A week after the arrrival of the relief column Robert and John Lawrence started back for New York. The countryside was still full of the rumors and threats of Indians, and the trip was uncomfortable, slow and full of anxiety.

The party reached Dorchester only to find that it had been burned out several months before. There was very little to show where the town had been, apart from the stone slabs of the main street. Nothing depressed Robert more than the sight of the blackened foundations both of the cabin where he had received so much kindness from the Butterfields and the cabin where he and Henry Bentall had sat talking so often together. From one of the soldiers Robert learned, however, that a number of the townspeople had been saved and were living in another settlement. He continued to hope his friends were among them.

As they passed the place where the town gate had been he thought of the tall boy with the floppy hair who had called out to Calvin, Agatha and himself as they went in that day in April. He wondered if the boy had been asleep when the Indians arrived. Here, all too plain to see, was the picture of what would have happened at Fort Charles, but for the slightest pressure in their favor in the balance. These ruins had a strange air, too, of having looked this way for a very long time, as though the few charred remains of the town had been all that was left of some long-dead civilization. Robert was glad when they fell out of sight, but he continued to brood on them for some days afterward.

They came at last to New York. One night of sleeping in a bed of fresh linen and down-filled pillows; one morning of waking to the sound of voices and of wheels turning on cobbles in the street below, then of going down to a breakfast of hot coffee and warm cakes in a comfortable sunlit parlor made the wilderness of the Indians, of fire raids, night attacks and scalping seem as remote as China. By the time he had been a week in the town Robert could hardly believe the two ways of life existed in the same world. It was only when he took off his smart new black three-cornered hat and looked at himself in the mirror that his scalplock told him it was not so long ago that he had been an Indian himself, living in a longhouse and hunting all day in the wilderness. Thinking of the look on the hatter's face when he had removed Jacob's ancient hat to try on the new one, he laughed so hard, all on his own, that an anxious maid came up to inquire if anything was wrong.

John Lawrence's back pay had made rich men of them both, and they enjoyed their spell in the city, though John spent much of his time being prodded and given orders and counter-orders by different doctors, civil and military. He had been granted an extended sick leave. He was still in pain and could not put either foot to the ground. It would be a year, at the very least, the doctors agreed, before he was able to walk, and one of his legs had had to be reset after the clumsy attempts that had been made to fit the bones together at the fort.

At the same time John Lawrence was informed that he would be needed that autumn in London to give his account of what had happened before a Military Board of Inquiry looking into the disaster that had fallen on his regiment. He was anxious for Robert to come with him. It was obvious he would need Robert's help on the journey, and Robert wanted to go back. Only one thing had caused him to hesitate.

Walking about New York one day, he had chanced to hear two men talking. One had said quite distinctly to the other that there was no better ordinary or inn in the Colonies than Massey's.

"Which Massey?" Robert had been rude enough to ask the stranger.

"Which Massey? Why, Sailor Massey," the man had replied good naturedly. "Everyone knows Sailor Massey."

Robert had succeeded in gaining the address from them, and he set off at an undignified run in search of the place. Sure enough as he walked in through the door the first thing that met his eyes was the sight of his old friend standing at the end of a long dining room carving a huge baked ham.

"Good day to you, sir," Massey called down the room as he saw him. "Will you take a cut off this ham with me?"

"Not if it's got weevils in it," Robert called as loudly back.

"Weevils!" Massey said. "Weevils, by God!" Some of the customers at the tables tittered. Massey looked hard at Robert, then flung down his carvers and called behind him. "Come, Hannah, leave your kitchen, see what I've found for you. . . . Kestrel, you're welcome, you're welcome!"

Hannah came out, flung her arms around Robert and cried out, "Back from the dead are you—oh, for goodness sake!"

"I'd never have recognized you but for that bit about the weevils," Massey said. "You look more like an Indian chief than that poor pale creature you were when the fever left you."

"Well, Indian chief I very nearly am," Robert said, and to the consternation of a good many quiet diners he swept off his hat, bowed low and displayed his scalplock.

"Great ghosts!" Hannah said. "Why did you do that to yourself?"

"It's nothing but a bad haircut," Massey said. "Likely he got it the same way I got the red complexion on the one side of my face. Come, sit down, take your plate of food and tell us your adventures."

This he did.

That night they insisted on helping to move John Lawrence to their rooms, where Hannah took over the task of looking after him. Any payment they flatly refused. "We've felt badly, Hannah and I have, often," Massey said, "that we left you when we did. We say we'd no choice and perhaps we hadn't, since we had a job enough to get away ourselves; still it's left a nasty taste behind and we're both as glad as we can be now to see you and look after your friend—so don't tarnish a good thing with talk of money."

Since Massey was short-handed and the inn was as popular as the stranger had claimed it was, Robert gave him some help, especially in the evenings, serving on the tables and cleaning up afterward. More than once Massey had hinted that he needed someone like Robert permanently. "Perhaps it's not what you'd want, though it's a good life, I find. But consider, Robert, consider—there are a hundred things you could do here. You've proved yourself, heaven knows, and everywhere you turn in this country they need someone the likes of you. Do you suppose in the Old Country I could have been the owner and proprietor of my own ordinary like this, with the customers jabbing one another with their elbows to get to my tables? Then when I've a minute to spare

I've my silversmith's shop in the shed behind; they're talking of me already to be on the town council and I've interests in printing to top it all up. Why, another year or two like the last one and they'll ask me to be Governor."

Robert laughed.

"No, Robert, but be serious a minute and think hard on it. You know you're welcome—whatever you decide—to stay here with Hannah and me—aye, and for as long as you like!"

At the same time John Lawrence was pressing Robert to name the sailing day when they could start on their way back, and he was talking each night of the fight they would make against Robert's uncle.

In the end Robert decided he could not put off the matter any longer, and he told Massey and Hannah that he would be sailing with John Lawrence to England as soon as they could get a ship. The look of disappointment on both their faces was enough to make him wish heartily that he could say something to make the decision less unpleasant. "Well," said Massey, "you're right, I'm sure, for yourself, but remember it's here at our house you'll get a better welcome than anywhere else in the world, should you ever come back."

The seas, it was said, were full of French men-o'-war and privateers, war having at long last been declared after it had been raging for a year in the American wilderness and elsewhere. Robert had some difficulty in finding a couple of berths. In the end he had to leave the matter with one of the port officers, a friend of Massey's, who by bribery or influence secured him what they wanted. It was not until John Lawrence was safely aboard and comfortable in his cabin that Robert came on deck to discover that the captain of the ship was Captain Mask.

By careful maneuvering Robert managed to avoid meeting the Captain more than twice during the voyage. On each of the two occasions Captain Mask said he hoped the quarters were comfortable and that he'd be delighted, so he would, to take wine with the young gentlemen in his cabin—or in theirs, if that would be more convenient for the invalid—whenever it pleased them to do so. It pleased Robert not at all and he tried to forget both the invitation and the encounter as soon as he could. (I was fated, it seems, to take that trip back to England with Captain Mask he threatened me with on the day of the sale two years ago, Robert thought to himself. At least Captain Mask knows nothing of this.)

Eight weeks after they left New York they first came in sight of England. At the same time, however, a sail was seen by the lookout. In no time a French privateer bore down on them. If it had not been for a very quick and professional display of seamanship on the Captain's part they might have found themselves in the hulks at Le Havre. This Captain Mask reminded them of a day later when they put in at Bristol. However, grateful though he was, Robert felt no wish to give the Captain the customary present, and thus they landed as soon as possible. Robert booked two places on the coach for London, and they were off in the early hours of the following morning.

As they rolled through the lush green parkland, the trees now turning yellow with autumn, and changed horses or stopped overnight in the small towns of red and white houses that looked as though they had been there, placid and trim and neat since the world began, Robert started to feel all the pleasant shocks of rediscovering something familiar after it has been given up for lost. And given it up he had—he had despaired of ever coming back to England. Now it seemed the most natural thing in the world that he should be there. For the first time since he lay in the bunk in the hold of *The Charming Betty* he tried to remember each room at the Hall. His excitement mounted with every milestone they passed. He half expected at each turning of the road to find the Hall there waiting for him. He had to keep telling himself he was hundreds of miles from it still.

20

The Landowner

THEY WERE DELAYED for several weeks in London. It was
necessary for John Lawrence to attend the military Court of
Inquiry into the defeat and massacre of the column, and,
though this dragged on, Robert, wanting his friend's support
and knowing he was as anxious as Robert to be there when
he reached the Hall, refused to go on without him.

While they waited they lived with Mr. Lawrence, who
made Robert almost as welcome as his own son. The lawyer
promised to come with them and in the meanwhile he wrote
three letters addressed to Thomas Entrick and three to his
attorney in Bower. There was no reply to any of these.

It was late in November when they finally set off, but the
weather was dry. They made good time as far as Chester.
Here they began a cross-country trip in slow wagons along
bad roads, spending several days progressing very little distance between small country towns.

At last, one bright afternoon in the first week in December,
the three of them arrived before the big bow window of
The Loyalist in the High Street, Bower. The hostlers helped
to carry John Lawrence to the inglenook by the fire. The
others saw their luggage attended to and ordered two horses
and a light cart for the next morning. "How I wish I could
ride!" John Lawrence said. "We'd make a far more imposing
attack on the Hall—a cart indeed!"

Mr. Lawrence went in search of the attorney's office, but

returned a quarter of an hour later with the news that it was closed and looked as though it had been locked up for a century. However, his obvious interest in the place had attracted an equal interest in some of the bystanders. After a while a shopkeeper had opened a conversation and soon he had promised to produce a lady who knew a good deal about the matter.

While he had been telling them this the lawyer had glanced at the wall of the taproom where a number of notices were posted up. "Hello, what's this?" he said. He lifted several of the Lost, Stolen or Strayed variety and announcements of Meets and Shows to uncover one of the notices, which had attracted his attention because the words "Tice Hall" had remained exposed.

"Here we are," he said, "here's a young fellow run off and nobody knows whether he's alive or dead." He snatched the piece of paper from the wall and came over to Robert.

But they had hardly time to read what had been written when a hostler came to tell them that there was a lady wishing to speak with them outside. Robert looked through the window to see someone he recognized at once. He hurried out and took each of Mrs. Jarrow's hands in one of his own and shook them vigorously. He would have thrown his arms around his uncle's housekeeper and kissed her, but she looked so startled and surprised he felt sure she had no idea who he was.

It took several minutes before he could make her believe it all. Even then she kept saying to herself, "Two years, is it only two years you've been gone? You look now like your father did when he first came back and he was already a soldier."

After he had made his introductions, Robert asked Mrs. Jarrow about his uncle and about the Hall. He learned that the Hall was empty and his uncle had left six months before.

"A strange thing it was," Mrs. Jarrow said. "I knew there was trouble of some sort about for him—visits in the middle of the night, and other nights with your uncle awake to all hours, walking about in that room of his he would let nobody into. Then one day I went to wake him and he was gone."

After that, she went on, there had been nothing but difficulties, the servants without their pay, the decision whether or not to shut up the house. Finally she had decided to move to Bower. "It was no good keeping the place open until he chose to ride back, and we'd lost hope of you long ago, Master Robert. Besides," she said, "in the end I wasn't sorry to make a change. First there was the sad time over you and then, though he was civil enough, your uncle, and fair to me in his way until the end, he never had a quiet conscience after your father got himself killed fighting. After you went it grew worse. No, he was a complicated one, and if I speak of him as dead that's—begging your pardon, Master Robert—how I think of him."

They started for the Hall on the following morning. A mile from their goal Robert left the others and went ahead on his own to complete the ride that had been interrupted two years before and to be the first to see the house. He rode at full gallop down the long, twisting drive, rounded the last turn and there was the Hall, gray gables, towers and out-buildings against the elm trees and the backdrop of gray hills. He galloped across the overgrown lawn and jumped a low wall and into a grass-grown court. At the door he sprang off the horse and turned the lock with the key Mrs. Jarrow had given him. The door creaked open; sunlight flooded into the darkness ahead. It's like a tomb, he thought, six months without light or air.

He walked through the front hall, his boots sounding on the floorboards, climbed the wide staircase, hallooed to a series of echoes down corridors with close-shuttered windows. All this was what he had wanted to do so often, he remembered, on the boat going to the Colonies and in the early months in the bleak New England winter, and yet—and yet he had never imagined the scene like this. What did it remind him of? Something quite different, yet strangely the same—the moment when he had broken through the tangle of cobweb and walked into the abandoned cabin in the wilderness. He felt a sudden wave of disappointment.

Voices sounded downstairs. He retraced his steps to the head of the stairs. His guests were waiting for him. Then he felt a certain return of his spirits. Well, he and Calvin had set to; they had worked hard and made the schoolmaster's old farm flourish. In the same way he could resurrect the Hall, make it better than it had ever been before, make it worthy of his return.

And so he did. He did not even wait for Mr. Lawrence to make his searches and to confirm that the deeds showed he was indeed the heir, though still, in law, a minor. No one questioned his claim. Nothing was heard of his uncle. He began that November. There was little money and most of what he did in those early, winter months he did with his own hands, clearing and putting right, as he had done before, on Calvin's first farm that bitterly cold winter and, later, on the second farm in the wilderness. As one year passed and then another he saw his work bear fruit, more slowly perhaps, but more certain of harvest than it had been before.

John Lawrence came to stay with him for his month's leave before he embarked under General Wolfe for Quebec and the west once more. They walked about the house and the grounds, his friend showing no more now than a slight limp as they stepped out together. Robert explained what he had done and what he intended to do. In the evenings they sat in the library and talked of the lands to which John Lawrence was returning. Then Robert, gazing into the flames of the fire, thought again of the wilderness and saw in those flaring reds and yellows the fresh warpaint of the Indians, the scarlet coats of the column of soldiers and, above all, the colors of the trees as he had glided past them on those autumn evenings on his raft. He remembered he had another property in the world, one to which Calvin had made him his heir just as surely as his father had made him heir to the Hall. He wondered why it was that he felt the same feeling at that moment for the meadow, the burned cabin and the stream that he had once felt for this house, to which, after all those wanderings, he had at last come home.